FROM LARRY WIGHTMAN

8-2-02

R. G. Cordes

The
Simple
Nature
of Existence

The
Simple
Nature
of Existence

LAWRANCE WIGHTMAN

American Literary Press, Inc.
Five Star Special Edition
Baltimore, Maryland

The Simple Nature of Existence

Library of Congress
Cataloging in Publication Data
ISBN 1-56167-544-X

Library of Congress Card Catalog Number:
99-091299

Published by

American Literary Press, Inc.
Five Star Special Edition
8019 Belair Road, Suite 10
Baltimore, Maryland 21236

Manufactured in the United States of America

Table of Contents
Chapters

Figures & Charts

Introduction
The Simple Nature of Existence

This is not a text book; there are no problems and no tests. This book is written to satisfy your curiosity about the mysteries of existence. You will find the solutions to these mysteries to be exciting amazing and fun to read about. This is the only book where you can find the answers to the mysteries of existence without any effort on your part. Everything is explained without any challenge to your problem solving ability.

Besides being fun to read this book will make you more intelligent than your associates unless they have also read it. This book will attempt to explain words you might not understand. For instance, in this case, intelligence means You will have more knowledge, understanding and awareness of the "Simple Nature of Existence" than any one else in the world except a few scientists. These few scientists, and those who have gone before them, have discovered "What" existence is and "How" it works. Their discoveries consists of what they have been able to prove to be true about existence. Note that scientific discoveries consist of what is proved to be true by extensive testing for truth, not by theory or verbal proclamation. It is very important for all of us to realize the basic difference between what any one says and what can be proven by tests.

Up until one hundred years ago very little truth was known about existence. Much was written and said about existence, but it was almost all wrong. We will not dwell on the wrongs of the past. In the last one hundred years, scientists have discovered, by test, many times more truth about existence than there was ever known before and they have written about it in great detail. However, almost no one has read what the scientists have written except other scientists. The number of true scientists in the world is negligible compared to the numbers of people. True scientists have found out "What" existence is and "How" it works. Engineers, business people, executives, doctors, politicians, lawyers, transportation people, etc., do not know "What" existence is or "How" it works. Existence is not complicated or difficult to understand but it has not been made readily understandable by scientists.

I did not read what scientists had written until I retired from doing engineering work all my life. That is when I wished I had known "What" existence was and "How" it worked when I was young. However, when I was young, there was very little such information available and it was not taught in school. This has not changed very much and this is a basic reason I have written this book. There is no other source for today's up to date information on "The Simple Nature of Existence." It is written so that anyone can understand it.

Chapter 1
Easy to Understand

This book includes data and charts in a completely understandable form so that the information is simply available if it is of interest. You don't have to study or remember any of it to understand the book. It contains some basic simple equations which are completely worked out with the solutions so you do not have to do any kind of mathematics or study to understand the book. It explains how simple equations work in case you are interested but that is not necessary to understand the book either.

Because the educational systems of the world today have left humans with an unsatisfied desire to know "The Simple Nature of Existence," this book was written to satisfy that desire without more school, without tests, without more instruction and without spending excessive time. However, this book will not replace education, in that it does not tell how to use a knowledge of existence to create physical changes as with engineering or chemistry and the like. But this book will make further education much easier to understand and it will furnish enlightenment that present education will not furnish.

Signs, Equations, Area, and Solutions

To refresh your memory or for your information if you wish, the following are the simplest forms of mathematics shown. You will not use them but you should recognize them when you see them. They include equations, signs of addition, subtraction, multiplication, division, squares and square roots.

An equation sign equals = always means that whatever is on one side of the sign equals whatever is on the other side. For instance:

2 + 2 = 4 defines a plus sign for addition
4 - 2 = 2 defines a minus sign for subtraction
2 X 3 = 6 defines a times sign for multiplication
6/3 = 2 defines a divide sign for division
2 squared = 2 X 2 = 2^2 = 4 defines square
4 square root = $\sqrt{4}$ = $4^{1/2}$ = 2 defines square root

You will note that the square and square root can be indicated by the small "2" and "1/2". These are called exponents. An exponent is a number which tells us how many times to multiply another number by itself in which case it is called a power. If it is a "2" it is a square, if it is a "3" it is a cube, a "4" a fourth power, a "5" a fifth power, etc.. For as high as you wish to go. Now, if an exponent is a fraction like "1/2", "1/3" or "1/4" etc. it is the inverse of a power. It means a number which is a square root, a cube root, a fourth root, etc., of the number. Now, there is one more thing about an exponent sign in front of it, that means that the number is a devisor, power and must go below the line. So that you will know what line, here is an example:

2 = 4 X $4^{-\frac{1}{2}}$ or 2 = 4/$4^{\frac{1}{2}}$ or 2 = 4/2 or 2 = 2

The line can be horizontal or slanting as shown.

A further review covers the determination of area, volume and the Pythagorean rule covered in Fig 11. Then finally we come to extremely large numbers encountered in discussions of the universe and extremely small numbers encountered in discussions of the atoms. Using extremely large and small numbers is made quite simple by the use of exponents called the powers of ten which is the next subject.

Area and Volume

So you don't have to remember

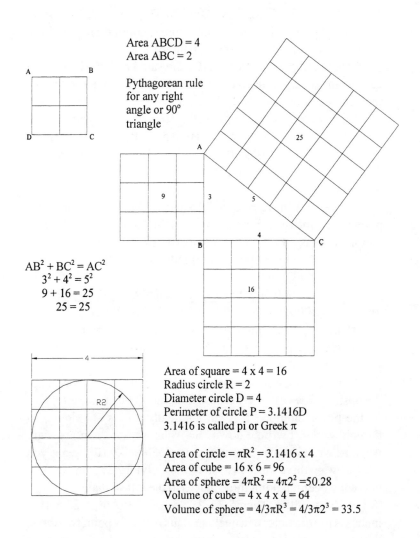

Area ABCD = 4
Area ABC = 2

Pythagorean rule for any right angle or 90° triangle

$$AB^2 + BC^2 = AC^2$$
$$3^2 + 4^2 = 5^2$$
$$9 + 16 = 25$$
$$25 = 25$$

Area of square = 4 x 4 = 16
Radius circle R = 2
Diameter circle D = 4
Perimeter of circle P = 3.1416D
3.1416 is called pi or Greek π

Area of circle = πR^2 = 3.1416 x 4
Area of cube = 16 x 6 = 96
Area of sphere = $4\pi R^2 = 4\pi 2^2$ = 50.28
Volume of cube = 4 x 4 x 4 = 64
Volume of sphere = $4/3\pi R^3 = 4/3\pi 2^3$ = 33.5

Fig. 1

L. W. Wightman

Powers of Ten

You already know the following. Consider any number times ten.

5.7 x 10 = 57 Then, 57 x 10 = 570 Then, 570 x 10 =5,700

I multiplied 5.7 times 10 three times, count them; and I got 5,700. Now if I multiply 1 times 10 three times (1 x 10 x 10 x 10) I get 1000 and 5.7 x 1000 = 5,700 the same as before. So, you can say that every time you multiply something by 10 you move the decimal point one place to the right.

Now, instead of writing the 10 x 10 x 10 down, you can just say that $10 \times 10 = 10^2$ or ten squared and $10 \times 10 \times 10 = 10^3$ or 10 cubed. Then $10 \times 10 \times 10 \times 10 = 10^4$ or 10 to the fourth power. The little numbers which determines the power are called exponents.

So, we could have written; $5.7 \times 10^3 = 5700.0$ and the decimal point would move three places to the right. Now, we will see how simple and easy it is to write big numbers.

$$43,000 = 43 \text{ thousand} = 43 \times 10^3$$
$$43,000,000 = 43 \text{ million} = 43 \times 10^6$$
$$43,000,000,000 = 43 \text{ billion} = 43 \times 10^9$$
$$43,000,000,000,000 = 43 \text{ trillion} = 43 \times 10^{12}$$

3.114×10^{28} is the number of nucleons in a 115 pound person. This reads three point one, one four times ten to the twenty-eighth power. We will discuss nucleons later.

Now, let's look at extremely small amounts. You know about the positive power of ten because if we don't put a minus (-) sign on the power number, it is automatically a plus (+) sign even though we don't write it down. So when we want a minus sign, we must write it down. A minus power of ten like 10^{-3} means you divide by ten three times instead of multiplying. That means you move the decimal point three places to the left so that:

$5.7 \times 10^{-3} = .0057$ Then $5.7 \times 10^{-6} = .0000057$ or, 6.23×10^{-14} inches is the diameter of a nucleon. This reads six point two three, times ten to the minus fourteenth inches. We will discuss nucleons later.

Now we will be able to talk about electrons in atoms and the universe which are as small and as large as we get. However,

THE SIMPLE NATURE OF EXISTENCE

first we will start with the simplest complete description of what existence is.

Chapter 2
What Existence Is

Existence consists of (1) forces (2) motion (3) stuff (4) space (5) time. That's it. That is everything there is to existence. The Science of Existence has to do with <u>how</u> these five things react with each other and <u>how</u> these reactions can be measured.

As we talk about the strange scientific truth of <u>what</u> existence is and <u>how</u> it works, you will find it easy to understand. However, <u>why</u> existence exists in the way scientists find it to exist when they run experiments and make measurements, is completely unknown by scientists and by me. Existence could have been completely different. We can easily dream up many different <u>what's</u> and <u>how's</u> of existence. But it isn't any other way. Existence is as scientists find it to be and no other way. Now we will discuss <u>how</u> scientists find existence to be.

In this book there are no problems and no tests, but you should remember the five things which make up the <u>what</u> of existence. An easy way to remember is, forces moving stuff through space in time.

Let's talk about stuff and space first. Stuff is made of atoms which come in various sizes numbered from one through ninety-two. All 92 atoms have names and numbers so you can tell them apart. Each different atom is also called an element because it can not be divided into anything smaller in any natural way on earth. Some atom elements you are probably familiar with are iron and aluminum which are called metals and are solid; mercury, a metal which is liquid and oxygen, a gas. All of the atoms of all the elements never touch each other, so you can call what is between the atoms space.

Now we know that stuff is nothing but atoms and there is no other kind of stuff, so let's talk about atoms. Atoms are made of extremely small electrons on the outside and a nucleus on the inside. (Note that NUCLEUS is not spelled NUCULUS.) The nucleus is made of protons and neutrons which are each about 1,836 times heavier than an electron. Protons and neutrons are essentially the same size. The only difference is that neutrons have an electron included which makes them neutral. Since protons and neutrons make up the nucleus of atoms, they are both called nucleons. All the electrons, protons, and neutrons inside the atoms never touch each other, so you can call what is between them space too.

The space within the atoms and the space between the atoms is all the space there is. Space seems to be nothing so it can't be moving, and yet we know that the earth is going around relative to the sun and the space around us seems to be going with us. But since it seems to be nothing, it is neither going with us or staying with the sun. Since space is like nothing, we can make it whatever we like. We can say the space around us is going as fast as we are in a train, an automobile, an aeroplane, or whatever. We can even say the space is standing still with respect to the enclosure which we are on or inside. So really, it is our immediate surroundings that we determine to be the so called stationary condition of space, not space itself, and our surroundings are all atoms and forces and nothing else.

Forces, Motion, Direction, and Time

Now that we know something about stuff and space, we will go on to forces, motion, and time. We can't talk about forces without talking about motion and we can't talk about motion without talking about time. We can't talk about forces, motion, or time without talking about stuff or atoms because without atoms, there could be no evidence of forces, motion, or time in today's existence.

The forces we are familiar with are those that result from so called touching things. We pick a book off a table. We drop it and it hits our foot. We drive a nail into wood. We pull the nail back out. We sharpen a pencil. All these uses of force have to do with pushing, pulling, twisting, hitting, or slicing. It seems that the touching of atom against atom must surely take place. Yet the forces of nature say differently. There are four forces of nature that scientists have been able to describe and measure to some extent.

The description and measurement of these four forces is determined by the affect these four forces have on atoms and the protons, neutrons, and electrons of which these atoms are made. The affect these four forces have takes place in the direction of attraction or repulsion from a distance, never by touching. Attraction is like pulling and repulsion is like pushing. As you will see, the touching we think we do is the result of very high forces operating from extremely short distances on the electrons of our atoms. If touching took place the atom's structure would be changed and they would cease to be the same elements. This does not happen at earthly temperatures.

The affect the four forces have is determined only by the motion of the atoms and their parts, the protons, neutrons, and electrons. When the four forces move the atoms and their parts, their motion is determined by their change in location with respect to one another in time.

The four forces of nature are called (1) the strong forces (2) the weak forces (3) the electromagnetic forces and (4) gravity. These four forces make existence the way it is. The *strong* force and the *weak* force operate on the protons and neutrons inside the nucleus of atoms and nowhere else. The *electromagnetic* forces operate between the protons in the nucleus and the electrons in an atom; they operate between the electrons in their atom; they operate between the electrons in their atom and the electrons in every other atom; and they operate between the electrons in their atom and the protons in every other atom. This seems complicated but it will be simple and clear shortly. The *gravity* force operates attractively only between all *atoms* and, as you will see later, between atoms and light.

To make the operation of the four forces simple and clear, we must describe the direction, the amount, and the distance over which the forces operate. First, let's establish the direction of the *electromagnetic* forces.

(1) The protons repel each other and attract all electrons.

(2) The neutrons do not repel or attract anything.

(3) The electrons repel each other and attract all protons.

These repulsion and attraction forces are equal for protons and electrons and are inversely proportional to the square of the distance between them: inversely means the greater the distance, the smaller the force.

Two protons repelling:

Two electrons repelling:

A proton and an electron attracting:

The closer they are together, the greater is the force of attraction or repulsion, whichever; and the farther apart they are, the less the force which is inversely proportional to the square of the distance between.

In books on electricity you will find the electron force of attraction for a proton called a negative charge and the force of attraction of a proton for an electron a positive charge. Since no electron exists without a so called negative charge and no proton exists without a so called positive charge there is no longer any reason to continue with this charge concept. It is a hold over concept which is more confusing than helpful, since it is backwards like the direction of current flows. Wherever an atom has more electrons than protons, it is said to have a negative charge and when an atom has fewer electrons than protons it is said to have a positive charge. Therefore, this book will not use the term charge and you will not miss it.

The gravity force is the simplest of all. Gravity is a force of attraction only. It operates between everything over infinite distance inversely as the square of the distance.

Right away you can see a problem here because the protons in the nucleus repel each other so the protons should fly apart, but they don't. That is the job of the *strong force* in the nucleus to hold the protons and the neutrons together in the nucleus without their touching. But the strong force is limited to the nucleus and does not act beyond the diameter of the nucleus.

The *weak force* is even more limited. It holds the protons and neutrons themselves together and does not act much beyond them. It has to do with the neutrons losing one electron and becoming a proton which is not very common and not worth considering in this book. It does indicate that a proton and a neutron are the same except a neutron includes an electron and therefore does not attract electrons or repel protons.

This strong force and weak force discussion is certainly not complete or totally correct, but it will have to do until you wish to study nuclear physics. Then you will find out what scientists have learned with nuclear accelerators since about 1960. You will find that protons and neutrons can be broken down into smaller parts called quarks which are controlled by many forces or particles with very strange names.

Up until now the forces have been simple to understand and easy to explain so now we will consider the motion of the atoms and the protons, neutrons, and electrons out of which they are made. These are the only things in existence that move except cosmic rays which rarely strike the earth except on mountain tops. But while the protons, neutrons, and electrons are the only things that move, they always move. So in existence there is no such thing as stationary even though it seems so. To talk about motion we must consider a change in the distance between two point locations either closer or farther apart. The direction of one point location relative to one other point location can be only toward or away. Therefore, the direction of a point location must be relative to enough other point locations to establish a so called stationary space. A point location can not spin as a location might. Direction becomes rather complicated when we consider all the various kinds of motion possible. The motion of one point location relative to another point location in a space determined by other point locations on many things can be toward, away, up, down, right, or left or any combination of these relative to all the other point locations which determine the so-called stationary space. The so-called stationary space seems to be moving around with the earth, which is moving around the sun, which is moving around with the Milky Way galaxy, which is moving away from all the other clusters of galaxies. So again, we say space is that in which all stuff, forces, and time exist.

To get some idea of the relative speed of stuff, the earth goes around the sun at 18.5 miles per second and the surface of the earth goes around at .3 miles per second, so the fastest you go around the sun is 18.5 + .3 = 18.8 miles per second which is pretty stationary compared to the speed of radiation force at 186,000 miles per second. Some kinds of motion are straight line, curved, wavy, spiral, vibrating, rotating around an internal axis, rotating around an external axis, and a combination of any or all of the above. Makes you dizzy doesn't it?

To have some way to talk about the relation of forces moving stuff through space in time, scientists have established what is called a coordinate system and as usual goofed it up. The coordinate system of a plane like a baseball field is called two dimensional and all of space is called three dimensional. Now, a dimension has to do with only *distance* in any direction so these coordinate systems should be called two directional and three directional systems. The two directions are one which is left and right direction called the "X" coordinate and two the forward and backward direction called the "Z" coordinate. The third coordinate is the up and down direction called the "Y" coordinate.

Now you will notice that when you go from right to left or from forward to backward or from up to down you go by a change of direction point. Therefore, scientists have decided that when you go right you go positive, left you go negative, forward you go positive, backward negative, up you go positive and down you go negative. That doesn't mean that negative is less than nothing it just means the other direction from positive. There is no such thing as less than nothing, no matter what scientists say, but it could mean you are in debt.

The coordinate system has three directions from a point in space or within a substance. But a point by itself is meaningless except as one end of a measurement or a distance of a dimension. When a point is used for such a purpose, it is also one end of a time called a start from where time can be measured the same as distance. Any measurement must be through time as well as space. Therefore, a coordinate system must consist of three directions in time as well as space. Scientists call this a four dimensional coordinate system with the inclusion of time.

Units of Distance, Direction, and Time

To talk further about motion we must have some units of measurement of the distance one location moves from another location. We must have at least two locations to measure distance, but if we can determine direction, that's no problem. The units of distance can be anything we want them to be as long as we agree on them. The units of distances are different around the world, but all of them can be converted into the others. We will use inches, feet , yards, and miles which are USA units. That's the length of a thumb joint, the length of a foot and from the nose to the tip of an outstretched hand. Pretty stupid units.

Then we must have some units of measurement of time so we measure how long it takes a location to go the distance we measured. For time we have a completely arbitrary division of the rotation of the earth relative to the sun divided into 24 parts called hours. This division could be 20 hours so that we had 10 hours A.M. and 10 hours P.M., each with 100 minutes and each minute with 100 seconds. Tens and hundreds are much easier to use than twelves and sixties. Oh well, you can correct time. I am too old to bother.

Now that we have units of distance and time, in some direction, we can determine the amount of distance per unit of time in that direction by simple division and we know how fast the average motion of the location was when it went from one location to another. We say average motion in a direction because we do not know how fast the location was moving before we started measurement of distance, during measurement or after measurement. If the time were very, very short then we can say that however fast the location went, it's speed didn't change much so the average that didn't change was it's speed or velocity. The location could move at a constant velocity or it could change to a higher or lower velocity. If it changes to a higher velocity we say it accelerates or to a lower velocity it decelerates. We say moving location in a direction to indicate a point motion rather than several points on a thing.

Chapter 3
The Nothing in Little Old Atoms

Now that we have the knowledge that stuff is made of atoms and that atoms are made of protons, neutrons, and electrons and that they are all moving in space but held together by forces, we should consider the configuration of an atom. How large are the parts of an atom, how much do the parts weigh, where are the electrons located around the nucleus, how far are the electrons from the nucleus, how are the electrons arranged around the nucleus, and just how large are atoms? Have you ever wondered about these things? Probably not, but you are wondering now and the answers will astound you. The answers will be like nothing you've ever dreamed of.

The different sizes of atoms from one to ninety-two start with number one having one proton which is the nucleus and one electron. Then comes two which has two protons and two neutrons in the nucleus and two electrons outside the nucleus. From then on, through number 92, each atom has successively one more proton and one or more neutrons in the nucleus. All atoms have the same number of electrons as protons and most have more neutrons than protons. All the atoms and a description of each are given on a chart called:

The Periodic Chart of the Atoms

There are various forms of periodic charts, but they all have more or less the same information. These charts should be available in your school. If not, you should see that your school principal makes them available. A very simple chart can be found in a dictionary under, "periodic." (They are available at Sargent Welch Scientific Co., PO Box 1026, Shokie, IL 60077. A booklet

Cat. No. 818808 explains everything on the chart.) You will find that these charts have more than 92 atom elements but that all those elements above 92 are man made and do not exist in nature. All those except plutonium have no use yet and have short life times because of radiant decay. Further, elements number 43 and 61 do not exist on earth. Elements 84 and 89 and element 91 only exist as radiant decay products of elements 90 and 92. This information about missing elements is of no importance in our discussion of existence but hardly anyone knows about it.

The knowledge of atomic measurements has been obtained by scientists over the years by various means using the spectrometer analysis of the characteristic spectra of the elements, Avogadro's law, X-ray diffraction, electron scattering, and bulk measurements which have resulted in the Periodic Chart previously mentioned. The measurements have resulted in the following values:

	Radius	Weight
Neutron	3.15×10^{-14} in.	3.7×10^{-27} lbs.
Proton	3.15×10^{-14} in.	3.7×10^{-27} lbs.
Electron	~~$.26 \times 10^{-14}$ in.~~	2.0×10^{-32} lbs.

Then there are $1/3.7 \times 10^{27} = 2.7 \times 10^{26}$ protons/ lb.

	Volume
Neutron	1.3×10^{-40} in.^{3}
Proton	1.3×10^{-40} in.^{3}
Electron	1.09×10^{-42} in.^{3}

Weight of one nucleon = 1836 electrons.

That is the easy part. Now the diameter of atoms is the tricky part and the amazing part. For one thing, they are all different and they all changed diameters some what all the time. So first we will talk about some diameters given in the *Periodic Chart of Atoms*:

Number	Atom	Diameter x 10^{-9} in.	Outer Shell Electrons
1	Hydrogen	6.22	1
2	Helium	3.86	2
3	Lithium	16.14	1
6	Carbon	7.17	4
8	Oxygen	5.12	6
9	Fluorine	4.49	7
10	Neon	4.02	8
11	Sodium	17.56	1
14	Silicon	11.50	4
18	Argon	6.93	8
19	Potassium	21.81	1
20	Calcium	18.11	2

From atom number 20, Calcium, on the electrons are not added to the atoms in an orderly progression. The structure of the progression, as one more proton, and one or more neutrons, and one more electron are added to make each succeeding atom is to have the electrons surround the nucleus in seven shells of an increasing number of electrons. We will say seven shells, however, except for the first shell, "K," which is just one shell "1s" the rest of the shells are actually groups of shells. The second shell "L" is a group of two shells "2s and 2p." The third shell "M" is actually three shells, "3s, 3p, and 3d." The fourth shell, "N," is actually four shells, "4s, 4p, 4d, and 4f." The fifth shell "O" is again "5s, 5p, 5d and 5f". The sixth shell, "P," is four shells again, "6s, 6p, 6d, and 6f." The seventh shell, "Q," doesn't have enough electrons to bother with. While the atomic shells are shown in scientific literature on a plain sheet of paper, they are supposedly in spheres where electrons spin, orbit, and vibrate faster as their distance from the nucleus increases. This is difficult to visualize so scientists say, don't try. I keep trying and failing.

The number of electrons in each succeeding shell turns out to be:

Shell No.	No. Of Electrons	Shell Letter
shell one	2 electrons	K
shell two	8 electrons	L
shell three	18 electrons	M

shell four	32 electrons	N
shell five	21 electrons	O
shell six	9 electrons	P
shell seven	2 electrons	Q

for Uranium, the heaviest element.

However, nature has established a rule that no element should have more than eight electrons in it's outer shell. Therefore on the way from Hydrogen to Uranium, whenever an outer shell gets eight electrons, a new shell is started. If this proceeded then no shell would have more than eight electrons. Therefore after shell three got eight electrons and shell four was started with two electrons (atom 20), further additional electrons were added to shell three until it got 18 electrons. Only then did shell four get more electrons until it got its eight electrons. When shell five was started, it got two electrons, further additional electrons were added to shell four until it got 18 electrons, then shell five got its eight electrons and shell six was started. When shell six got two electrons, shell four, not shell five, began to get more electrons until it got 32 electrons. Only then did shell 5 begin to get more electrons until it got 18 electrons at atom 79, Gold. Then shell six began to get more electrons until it got its eight at atom 86, Radon. Then the final shell, seven, was started and when it got two electrons shell six began to get more electrons. Shell five stayed at 18 electrons and shell six stayed at 8 until atom 89 when shell six went to nine electrons, then shell five increased to 21 electrons at atom 92, Uranium. Sometimes an outer shell will have only one electron while an inner shell will receive two electrons, but not often. Now how does this increase in the number of electrons affect the diameter of an atom? Not at all the way you would think. Chart #1 shows how the number of electrons affects the diameter of atoms compared to the electromagnetic attraction between the electrons and protons.

CHART 1

Diameter of the atoms in the sequence of the Periodic Chart of the elements.

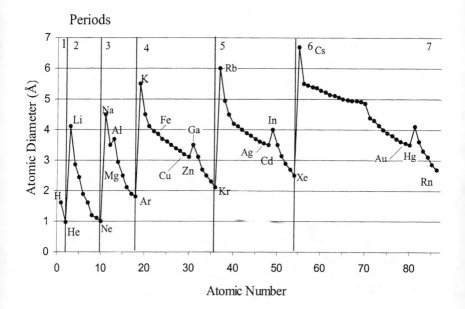

Number of elements in each period.

Each element is heavier than the one before by the weight of one electron, one proton, and one or more neutrons, except elements with a variable number of neutrons.

The smallest diameter elements are the noble gasses and the largest are the single valent electron atoms following the eight outer electron noble gasses.

Do not confuse the number of atoms which are in each period with the number of electrons which can be in each shell. There are seven periods and seven groups of shells.

The largest atom in the Periodic Chart is number 55, Cesium, which is 26.30 x 10^{-9} in. in diameter and all the following atoms with more electrons are smaller. But don't let that fool you because all atoms have a tremendous diameter relative to the size of their parts.

The 3.86 x 10 in.$^{-9}$ diameter of a Helium atom is 3 x 10^4 times the diameter of its nucleus. The 13.54 x 10^{-9} in. diameter of an iron atom is 5.1 x 10^4 times the diameter of its nucleus. The 26.3 x 10^{-9} in. diameter of a Cesium atom is 8.19 x 10^4 times the diameter of its nucleus. Thus if a nucleus were one foot in diameter, the outer electrons would be 15,000 feet or 25,000 feet or 40,000 feet away for Helium, Iron, and Cesium. That is a radius of 2.8 miles, 4.3 miles, and 7.6 miles. The electrons would be about one quarter inch in diameter.

Atomic Solid Stuff

While the parts of atoms are almost non-existent in size and the electrons are so far apart that the atoms are almost absolutely space, the density of the parts is tremendous. A cubic inch of protons or neutrons would weigh 28.19 trillion pounds. You don't believe it do you? But it's true. Now, let's illustrate how dense the stuff of atoms is and how almost nothing they are at the same time. You will be amazed.

We talk about stuff as solid, liquid, and gas, but we really don't understand solid. Let's see what solid really is. Let's see what happens if we do away with all the forces except gravity and let the electrons join the protons to make neutrons so all the neutrons actually touch each other. We will consider the neutrons are spheres and we will force them into cubes of equal volume. Now we know how much things weigh so all we have to do is see what their volume will be. We will determine their volume to be a cube and we will see what the dimension of the side of the cube is.

Now that we have stuff made of nothing but neutrons, we will determine that their spherical volume is in cube as follows:

The volume of a sphere is $4/3\pi R^3$

Then we can say it is $4/3\ \pi\ (D/2)^3$

Where the D is the spherical diameter.

Then the volume will be $\dfrac{4\pi D^3}{3 \times 2^3}$

And that will be $.5236D^3$

Now the volume of a cube $= S^3$

Where S is one side of the cube. Then we can say the volume of the cube is equal to the volume of the sphere or $S^3 = .5236D^3$

Now if we take the cube root of both sides we see that $S = .806D$ for a cube of side S which has the same volume as a sphere of diameter D of a neutron. Therefore, a spherical neutron of a diameter D of 6.3×10^{-14} inches will have a cubic volume of $S^3 = .5236\ (6.3 \times 10^{-14})^3$ in^3 the neutron volume of S^3 is 13.1×10^{-42} in^3.

The neutron mass is 3.693×10^{-27} pounds so there are 2.7×10^{26} neutrons in one pound. Now we can take the volume of one neutron times the neutrons per pound and determine the volume of a pound of neutrons. This turns out to be $131 \times 10^{-42} \times 2.7 \times 10^{26} = 354 \times 10^{-16}$ in^3 or 354×10^{-16} cubic inches of neutrons per pound of anything truly solid.

Now let's take the pounds mass of three different sized things and see what the solid cubic volume is. First, a cubic foot of uranium with a mass of 1,170 pounds. So 1, 170 pounds at 3.54×10^{-16} cubic inches per pound amounts to 4.14×10^{-12} cubic inches. A cube this size would be .00075 inches on one side. That is invisible.

Since a cubic foot of uranium doesn't amount to much, let's assume that the human population of the earth either is or soon will be six billion humans and that their average weight is one hundred pounds. Then we have a total of 600 billion pounds of human with a neutron volume of 354×10^{-16} cubic inches per pound. That is a total $600 \times 10^9 \times 354 \times 10^{-16}$ cubic inches or .02124 cubic inches of humans which amounts to a cube which is .277 inches on a side. That is just a little larger than a one quarter inch cube so you can remember it.

As long as we have gone this far let's see how large the whole earth would be if it were really solid. The weight of the earth is

13.9 X 10^{24} pounds. So we can take 13.9 X 10^{24} pounds times the volume of one pound of neutron or 354 X 10^{-16} cubic inches per pound and we get a total volume of 4921 X 10^8 cubic inches. This is a cube 7,900 inches or 658 feet or 219.4 yards on a side. That is just a fair drive on a golf course.

If this really solid earth were a sphere instead of a cube, it would have a radius of 408 ft. compared to its original radius of 20.5x10^6 ft. This drastic decrease in the radius of the earth would cause a comparable increase in the gravity of the earth. This increase in gravity force would be inversely proportional to the square of these radii. That means that a 100 pound person on the present earth would weigh 100 $(20.5\times10^6/408)^2$ pounds on the surface of the solid earth. That amounts to .25x10^{12} pounds which is one quarter of a trillion pounds. Of course this solid person would be invisible. This tremendous increase in weight shows how great the force of gravity can be at shorter distances. It also shows how great the other three forces must be to keep the nucleons and electrons from actually touching each other so that stuff would actually be solid.

Now you should have a better idea about the meaning of solid or should you? Nuclear scientists have shown that neutrons are composed of three smaller parts called quarks which take up only about forty percent of the volume of a neutron. But we aren't going to become involved with nuclear stuff in this book, so this is as small as we go.

The whole purpose of looking at the really solid side of existence is to show that stuff is really mostly nothing but the forces which keep the nucleons and electrons spread very far apart so that there is about as much space inside an atom as outside. Therefore, when we talk about the motion of nucleons and electrons you will realize they have plenty of room in which to move even if they are heavy metals.

Now that we have some idea of the gravity force when the spherical mass is very high and the radius is very short, we should consider the condition of a star like the sun if it shrinks down to a radius where the light photons can no longer leave the outer surface. There is a name for this radius. It is called the Schwarzschild radius after a scientist by that name of course. To start with, any spherical mass will have an escape velocity "V" which will be:

G = gravitational constant
M = spherical mass

$$V = \left(\frac{2GM}{R}\right)^{1/2}$$

R = spherical radius

where Rsch = Schwarzchild R

From this:

M = Mass of the sum

$$Rsch = \frac{2GM}{C^2}$$

C = photon light velocity

Then:

Rsch = 9,843 ft. for the maximum radius of the Sun if it were a "Black Hole". This is greater than the radius of solid Sun, which is 3,795 ft. So after the sun emitted no photons and therefore became a "Black Hole" it could shrink much further before it became truly solid.

Chapter 4
Touching and Listening

Touching

Now maybe we have enough knowledge of atoms to talk about atoms touching or not touching. Shortly we'll talk about atoms combining to make molecules and compounds and substances like wood and stone and bones and machines etc. So you can do what is called touching any of these things. An ax must touch wood while chipping yet let's take a look at the atoms on the cutting edge of the ax and the surface of the chips cut. They have not changed a bit. They may have moved relative to some other atoms but they still have the same nucleus and the same electrons all moving just like before or maybe faster. So what happened. Scientist Richard Feynman shows a curve (shown in Fig. 2) which explains what happened.

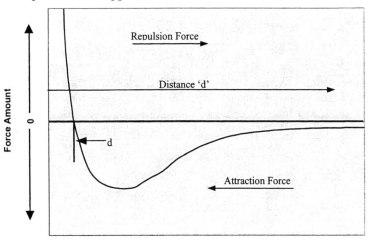

Fig. 2

The atoms attract each other when they are apart but when they get close enough for the electrons to be concerned at distance "d" the repulsive force will not be overcome. This atom will be pushed closer to another and many atoms may be moved but not touched.

This does not mean that impacts like billiard balls and bullets do not occur. It means that when they do occur the electrons of the atoms do not touch.

Sound

This arrangement of the atoms and molecules and the force between them is one of the most important concepts you should ponder because it causes most everything that happens. It causes the pressure of a gas in a container. It allows the molecules of liquids to slide over each other without coming apart. It allows all solids, even so-called brittle ones, to be flexible. These characteristics of stuff are the basis of what we call sound or noise, whether we hear it or not. We hear sound with our ears and we feel it with our skin but very low and very high frequency sound we can not feel at all. Sound frequency is the number of push and pulls on our ears or skin per unit of time.

When sounds vibrate like a bell we can both feel and hear it. What we hear is a change in air pressure against our ear drums. The change in air pressure is caused by the surface of the bell which vibrates because of its flexibility. And you know why it is flexible. Almost all materials transmit sound but the more brittle they are the better they transmit and the softer they are the worse they transmit. Glass transmits sound at 18, 050 feet per second, air at 1,100 feet per second, water at 1,460 feet per second, rubber at 177 feet per second if at all and vacuum at zero feet per second.

The flexibility of all stuff which produces sound has to do with increasing pressure (force per unit area) which causes a decrease in volume followed by a decrease in pressure which causes an increase in volume. This is the case for solids, liquids and gases.

The movement of sound is said to be in waves which are called mechanical waves or pressure waves as distinct from transverse waves. However, transverse string waves in musical instruments produce mechanical sound waves. The study of musical sound waves is far too detailed and complicated for this book.

Chapter 5
Heavy, Fast and Hot Stuff

Temperature and Velocity

Now let's talk about the movement of electrons and atoms all of which is the result of the forces, mainly the electro magnetic forces. When scientists measure this movement they call it temperature. The greater the amount and faster the movement the higher the temperature and visa versa. However, we must consider an exception to motion temperature proportionality where stuff goes though a change of state from a solid to a liquid to a gas or the reverse. During a change of state the arrangement of the atoms of the stuff changes so that the motion changes but the temperature remains constant. We will consider this exception later.

Gravity, Force, Acceleration, and Mass

The movement against a given amount of force for a given distance or the movement of a given amount of stuff at a given rate of movement or velocity results in a measurement scientists call *energy*. If the velocity is multiplied times the amount of stuff this presents a problem because you can divide a distance by a time to get a velocity but you don't know how to measure the amount of stuff. You can measure the stuff and get the volume and you can weigh it and get the pounds but that won't work in this case because the pounds are only the measure of the gravity force at the surface of the earth. As soon as you go to the top of a mountain or out in space, the gravity force in pounds will become smaller and smaller inversely proportional to the square of the distance from the center of the earth to the stuff. Inversely means that as the distance increases the gravity force gets smaller. So its obvious we need some way to measure the stuff so the measurement is the same no matter where the stuff is. There is a way to do this and scientists call this measurement *mass*. The *mass* of any stuff is the weight of the stuff at any distance from the center of the earth divided by the acceleration the force of gravity would give the stuff at that distance from the center of the earth. Now we know that acceleration is the increasing of the velocity of stuff. But the only way stuff can accelerate is if it is continually pushed by a force such as gravity in this case. Scientists have by experiment found out what the acceleration of a pound of stuff is at any distance form the center of the earth. So all we have to do is divide the number of pounds of stuff by what scientists have found the acceleration of that point to be and voila, we have the *mass*. Once we know the *mass* of our stuff, its *mass* will be the same anywhere in the universe. Why is that? Because as the distance from the center of the earth increases, the weight or force of gravity and the acceleration it creates decrease at the same rate so that the weight divided by the acceleration is always a constant for that particular piece of stuff.

What we have said here is that the mass of our stuff is equal to its weight which is the force of gravity divided by the acceleration which the force of gravity will cause. If we say the mass is M and the force of gravity is F and the acceleration it causes is A then;

$M = F/A$ or F=MA   MA is same as M x A

or force equals mass times acceleration.

This is one of the basic rules of nature. So from now on any time we talk about stuff we mean mass and anytime we say mass we mean stuff.

To get back to our starting point which was the measurement of energy, we can see that a force "F" can cause our mass "M" to accelerate from no velocity to some velocity and then to a higher velocity. If at any velocity we take away the force "F", our mass will just keep going at that velocity forever unless we put another force on it to make it go faster or to slow it down. The velocity of our mass which is some distance "D" divided by the time "T" it takes to go that distance, depends on the force "F" that made it accelerate to that velocity from when it had no velocity. If our mass accelerates from no velocity to some velocity V, its average velocity was V/2. Therefore the distance it goes to get to "V" velocity is $D = \frac{1}{2} VT$ and the acceleration is $A = V/T$ or the final velocity $V = AT$. If we put the AT where the V is in $D = \frac{1}{2} VT$ it becomes $D = \frac{1}{2} ATT$ or $\frac{1}{2} AT^2$. If we say that the energy "E" is equal to the work the force "F" does to move our mass "M" through the distance "D" or $E = FD$, then we can say $E = F \times \frac{1}{2} AT^2$. Since $F = MA$ we can say that energy $E = MA \times \frac{1}{2} AT^2$ or $E = \frac{1}{2} MA^2 T^2$. Then since $V = AT$ we can say:

Energy $E = \frac{1}{2} MV^2$ as well as FD.

Textbooks will refer to the energy measured by multiplying a force by the distance the force is applied as work. But work equals energy. If after our M gets to velocity V, a force makes it accelerate to a higher velocity Vh we can find the increase in energy Ei by finding Eh and subtracting E. The subtraction will look like this:

E   high $Eh = \frac{1}{2} MV_h^2$ so $Ei = Eh-E$

E   increase $Ei = \frac{1}{2} MV_h^2 - \frac{1}{2} MV^2$ or $1/2 M(V_h^2 - V^2)$

As long as our mass M goes along at velocity V it is not gaining or losing any energy from a force. However, our mass M has the potential of producing a force by slowing down or decelerating and there by giving up some or all of its potential energy depending on how much our mass M decelerates. A large mass going slowly can have the same energy as a small mass going fast. What we have been doing here is kind of like algebra and you may not know how to do algebra yet but if you get the idea that energy is the condition of stuff when it moves, that will do. Energy measures the reaction of force on stuff when the force makes the stuff move. Energy is not a thing, it is simply the product of two things, stuff and motion. Remember that.

This is a long way around, but it is the scientists way of measuring the amount of *Kinetic Energy* our mass "M" has when it moves at velocity "V." The word Kinetic means it is moving.

The other kind of energy scientists talk about is *Potential Energy*. That means our mass "M" hasn't done anything yet but it might. If our mass "M" is setting on top of a partly open door it has *Potential Energy* which, if someone opens the door it becomes *Kinetic Energy* by the time it hits them on the head.

You knew we were going to hit someone on the head, didn't you? The *Potential Energy* force in this case came from gravity but it could come from a stretched spring, gun powder, gasoline or any potential source of force like electro magnetic force.

So now you have some knowledge of what energy is that we pay for when we pay the gas bill, the electric bill and when we buy gasoline. You don't think there is too much connection do you?

Energy in General

Let's look at energy in a more general way. No matter how we measure energy, all it amounts to is the motion of stuff and you know what stuff is. You know the atoms and their nucleons and electrons are always in motion so they always have energy. You know that the basic measure of their motion is temperature. The temperature of our mass M is a direct measure of its heat except for the so called *Latent* heat energy required for a change of state from a solid to a liquid or from a liquid to a gas. This change of state takes place without any temperature change because the energy is absorbed or given up by a change in the bonding force between the atoms or molecules rather than a change in their motion. Heat energy is exactly the same as kinetic or potential energy and their measurements can be interchanged.

To be sure we keep our thinking straight, when we talk about motion, we are talking about velocity and or acceleration in some direction without regard to what or how much is moving. When we talk about the motion of a given mass we are talking about energy of some kind. Temperature has to do only with the motion of atoms and their parts, not with what the stuff is or how much of it there is.

In the beginning we talked about the simple nature of existence consisting of forces moving stuff through space and time. Now we have just covered forces moving or accelerating stuff or mass through space in time and called the result energy. So you see the simple nature of existence is called energy. Without it, we do not exist.

Everything we have said about finding the amount of forces, the amount of motion as in velocity or acceleration, the amount of the stuff or mass in an amount of time is true and usable as long as the velocity of the motion is low compared to the velocity of radiation or light which is 186,000 miles per second. So as long as you stay under 1,000 miles per second don't worry about it. However, even then your time will slow down a little, the distance will be a little shorter and your mass will be a little greater but you won't notice it. We will explain more about this later.

Temperature Scales

Now that we are considering temperature we had better consider the problem we have gotten ourselves into with measurements. There are two basic systems of measurement. An archaic system which we still use called the English system and a more scientific system called the Metric system. The English system uses inches, feet, yards, ounces, pounds and Fahrenheit degrees with water boiling at 212 degrees and freezing at 32 degrees. The metric system uses centimeters, meters, kilometers, grams, kilograms and Celsius degrees with water boiling at 100 degrees and freezing at 0 degrees. In the metric system the units are multiples of 10 while in the English system they are not. Both systems have an absolute temperature scale for measuring temperatures above absolute zero which is the lowest temperature there can be. Atoms and their parts still move when at absolute zero but they do not radiate. Above absolute zero they do radiate.

Since temperature is the measure of the amount of motion the atoms and their parts have, the physical characteristics of atoms are pretty much controlled by their temperature. Most of our experience with the elements is from observations between the freezing and boiling temperature of water.

To keep these goofy temperature scales straight in your mind.

You may want to refer to chart 2.

	English			Metric		
	Fahrenheit	Difference	Rankine	Centigrade	Difference	Kelvin
Sun 10,340			10,800	5,727		6,000
		10,128			5,627	
Boil 212			672	100		373
		180			100	
Freeze 32			492	0		273
		492			273	
Abs. Zero -460			0	-273		0

Chart 2

You will notice that all the differences on the English side are 9/5 times the differences on the metric side and Rankine numbers are 9/5 times the Kelvin numbers. However, the Fahrenheit numbers are not 9/5 times the centigrade numbers, only their differences are.

Centrifugal Force and Gravity

Now to review and add a common force. We have talked about how a force will accelerate a mass and how scientists call that F=MA. We have covered the measurement of a force used to move a mass through a distance and scientist call that work or W=FD. We have said that work is energy and that we can measure the energy required to accelerate a mass to a velocity V which is E= ½MV². Now we need to know about how gravity can pull the moon toward the earth and the earth toward the sun and have them stay the same distance away. They do stay pretty much the same distance away.

Well, there is a force which pushes the moon away from the earth and pushes the earth away from the sun just the same amount as gravity pulls them together. This force is called centrifugal force. Centrifugal force is what holds the water in the bottom of a bucket if you swing it around and around on the end of a rope. If you let go of the rope the water bucket and all will fly off in a straight line. All the stuff that moves will move in a straight line unless a force changes its direction. Well, gravity is the force which changes the direction of the moon and the earth so they go in circles instead of straight lines. The gravity force which pulls them into circles is called centripetal force or the force which pulls toward the center. The force which would pull the moon and the earth out of a circle and back into a straight line is the centrifugal force and is equal to MV^2 divided R where M is the mass of the moon or the earth, V is their velocity around their circle and R is the radius of their circle. It looks like Fig. 3:

SPIRAL GALAXY

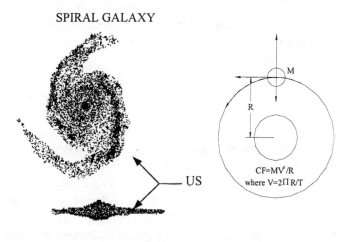

Fig. 3

Not only the moon, the earth and the sun are held in place in this manner, but our Milky Way galaxy and all other spiral galaxies in the universe are held together in this manner. A galaxy is a number of clumps of suns or stars in space. Beyond our Milky Way galaxy there are no stars until we get to another galaxy. Our galaxy has about 3×10^{11} stars within the radius of our sun from the center of our galaxy which is about two thirds of the way out form the center. You see our spiral galaxy is a disc with a lump in the center and long arms which curve back. Our sun is traveling around the center of our galaxy at 500,000 miles an hour and the galaxy is so large it will take 230 million years to make one revolution. Don't wait up. Our Milky Way is one of about 26 local galaxies which belong to a cluster.

Even so, the rotational speed of our Milky Way galaxy is much greater than the rotational speed necessary to balance the measured gravitational mass of our galaxy. This is true of all galaxies. Therefore, scientists believe there is additional mass in the universe which we can not detect. It is called Dark Mass and it is the subject of many scientific search programs. Even though all clusters of galaxies are moving away from each other, the simple nature of this force system of centrifugal force versus gravity is their nature of their existence.

So, just for fun, how much lighter do you think you are at the equator than at the poles where there is no centrifugal force. Unless I made a mistake you would be about .37 percent lighter. Not enough to bother with.

By now you may be thinking, what's so simple about the nature of existence. But now is the time when we should think about pondering. When I was young, I had a professor by the name of Hill and as we would walk along, he would encourage me to ponder things. To daydream seriously, to think things over forward and backward. To think slowly for awhile and then go on to something else, but to come back to the same subject later and ponder again. It's amazing how much more clearly you can think about things the second or third time around. Of course, it takes time but its more fun and a lot more profitable than television.

Now to get back to the centrifugal force balancing the gravity force. There is only one radius at which this happensand this is where the forces are equal or $MV^2/R=GMMe/R^2$ where G is the gravity proportionality constant, M is the body mass, Me is the earth mass and $V=2\pi R/T$ where T is the time of one revolution.

Then, $4\pi^2R^2/T^2=GMe/R$, the M's cancel

or $R^3=T^2GMe/4\pi^2$

or $R=\sqrt[3]{T^2GMe/4\pi^2}$

Where R equals the distance to a satellite, the moon, or from the sunto any planet if Me is the mass of the sun. Then, the radius of an earth satellite is 26,000 miles.

34

Chapter 6
What Radiation Really Is

Molecules and Valence

We have some knowledge of which elements are solids, liquids, or gases at what is called STP. This is standard temperature and pressure, which is about 32 degrees Fahrenheit and atmospheric pressure of 15 pound per square inch. However, all elements go from solid to liquid to gas if the temperature goes from absolute zero to as high as need be. But there are a few exceptions. Helium won't freeze and some elements go from solid to gas without becoming liquid. They sublime. Water expands when it freezes but in general atoms expand as their electrons move faster increasing their temperature, their energy, and their spacing. So far we have considered only atoms of elements except water which is a molecule made of three atoms of two elements, hydrogen and oxygen. The atoms of most elements prefer to combine with atoms of the same or other elements to form molecules. Molecules are two or more atoms of the same or different elements joined together by their electrons so that their nuclei (plural of nucleus) tend to claim some of the same electrons. When atoms join to make molecules, they are called a chemical compound like sugar, salt, rust, plastic, etc. Then different compounds go together to make substances like dirt, rocks, wood, skin, etc. How this all happens and its measurement is to a great extent called chemistry. You can learn about it in high school and beyond.

However, how atoms join to make molecules is based on what you already know about atoms. Remember all atoms never have more than eight electrons in their outer shell and that is the basis for making molecules out of atoms. If you ask me why atoms never have more than eight electrons in their outer shell; I'll say

I don't know and I don't think anyone else knows, so eight is the way it is. Also remember atoms have the same number of electrons as protons in the nucleus so they are balanced as far as electron to proton forces are concerned but some electrons are much farther from the protons than others in atoms with many electrons. So in up through atom 20, Calcium, the number of electrons in the outer shell determine how the atoms combine, but after that the electrons in the outer two shells often affect the combining number of electrons. They are called valence electrons. When atoms have one or two valence electrons or six or seven valence electrons in the outer shell, they can readily give up or take on one or two electrons. In this case they are called ions which means their proton electron forces are unbalanced. Thus, sodium with one electron in its outer shell readily joins with chlorine with seven electrons in its outer shell to make salt or sodium chloride plus a sodium ion.

However, all the atoms with all eight electrons in their outer shells are called noble and are gases. They don't readily join with any other atoms. They are Helium, Neon, Argon, Krypton, Xenon and Radon. Radon is atom number 84 and is very heavy but still a gas down to -80° Fahrenheit. Helium, the lightest noble gas stays a gas clear down to absolute zero temperature which is 460 degrees below zero Fahrenheit which is zero degrees Rankine, as you can see on the temperature chart.

Photon Force and Energy Transfer and Critical Frequency

So now that we have motion and temperature the same and energy and heat the same and atoms combining into molecules and compounds and substances, let's consider how all these are transferred one into the other. Science says that the one thing that is common about everything in existence is motion. Remember that existence is forces moving stuff through space in time. We know that forces make the motion of stuff per unit of time in space. But since existence has lasted a considerable amount of time with only a little apparent decrease in motion, we might think that motion is here to stay awhile. Since motion depends on force, how is it perpetuated? That means why does everything still constantly move.

Everything moves because there is a force which transfers motion or energy from electrons which move faster to electrons which move slower. If that is true why don't all electrons eventually move at the same speed? Well, maybe its because of the force of gravity or maybe they will someday. Until then let's talk about the force which transfers energy to keep everything moving. This force is called photons. Photons are transfer forces. They have no mass and therefore are not particles and have no energy based on the velocity of mass. They are forces which transfer energy by what is called radiation and at whatever frequency their sending electron imparted. In their textbooks, scientists say that photons are energy rather than that they transfer energy. Their energy is determined by a constant called "h" times their frequency as explained later. Photons are units of all radiation. All radiation is composed of photons. The fact that radiation is transferred at frequencies instead of a steady stream, is the basis of the Quantum Concept of physics. What ever energy a photon transfers was subtracted from the electron which sent it and will be added to the electron which absorbs it. Since the speed of photon transfer is constant at 186,000 miles per second in a vacuum, never more and never less, the amount of energy transferred is proportional to the photon frequency and to the number of photons per unit of cross sectional area. Photons in the frequency range from 1.5×10^{14} to 10^{15} cycles per second are called light. Since this frequency range is very small, most of the energy transfer by photons is invisible to our retina and was unknown until recently. Photons are electromagnetic force waves and transfer energy through frequencies from gamma, x-ray, ultra violet, light, infra red, microwave, radar, T.V., FM radio, short wave radio, AM radio and long waves which we know little about. Now isn't that interesting?

Since you and I are mostly nothing, photons of the lower frequencies go right through us as if we didn't exist which we almost don't. X-ray do too to some extent.

Now that we know that photons transfer energy, how do they do it? Remember we are transferring energy from a greater motion to a lesser motion but the motion produces various frequencies all at the same velocity. So we are talking about the frequency of motion. Now believe me, I have never seen an electron or even an atom so we will just have to consider what these scientists say. It is really quite simple. They use the words emit, deflect, reflect and absorb. To emit radiation means to put out photons. Photons are emitted by electrons in atoms, molecules and antennas as they decrease in frequency. Photons can be deflected or reflected from electrons. Photons are absorbed by the same means by which they are emitted by electrons according to their frequency.

Now just what do we mean by the frequency. Well everything in existence proceeds in time steady by jerks like sound. Since nothing really stands still, everything must move. Since everything must move, the motion must be either smooth or jerky. It's not smooth even when it seems to be. We can have a motion which successively goes and stops or goes fast then slow. The motion could vibrate back and forth and move at right angles to the vibration. The motion could spin around an axis and move along the axis. In all these cases the motion is successively repetitive and the frequency is the number of repetitions per unit of time. Each repetition is called a cycle so frequency is the cycles per unit of time. When we know both the frequency and the velocity, we can divide the velocity or distance per unit of time by the frequency and get the distance of each cycle. Instead of cycle length, scientists call this the wave length for photons because photons consist of two waves traveling along together. One is an electric force and the other is a magnetic force. These forces are transverse to the direction of the photon motion and at right angles to each other. Transverse means to cross at right angles.

The amount of energy which photons can transfer to a given area is determined by (a) the frequency of the photons, (b) the number of photons which strike the area per unit of time or the density of the photons. The energy transferred per unit of time is called the watts or horse power or any kind of energy per unit of time.

The frequency of the photons does not change in flight but the density of the photons depends on the distance from the source and the distribution at the source. For instance, white hot iron emits photons at a higher density at an angle to the surface rather than perpendicular to the surface. This is unusual, however. Laser photons fly about parallel or at constant density. The temperature reading of a temperature indicator is determined by the photons it receives from its ambient condition, ambient means surrounding. These photons can have both frequency and density variations which will increase or decrease the temperature reading until the photon absorption and reflection of the indicator equals its emission and the temperature reading remains constant again. If the temperature indicator medium is a liquid, its reading change will be caused by a change in the motion of the liquid atoms and electrons so that it expands or contracts.

For AM radio frequencies and 30 to 100 ft. wave lengths, an antenna must be used to produce the many photons required for long wave transmission. The antenna is generally about the wave length to be broadcast. The electrons oscillate up and down the antenna at the frequency of that wave length and emit photons of that frequency which transmit very little energy. They will however travel right through the atoms of most elements. They will transmit their energy to a receiving metal antenna. Here the power at the receiving frequency must be amplified by a separate power source to be heard. For long distance low frequency the wave length is miles long. For normal 60 cycle power lines the wave length is 3,000 miles. For F.M. radio and T.V. the wave length is about 3 to 10 ft., and for microwaves the wave length is a few inches.

As we have mentioned, at frequencies above infra red frequencies, are visible light frequencies, ultra violet frequencies and X-ray frequencies. Now what is there about the electrons in atoms and antennas that makes them emit all these frequencies of radiation? We know that the higher the frequency the faster the wave motion at the constant transfer velocity and the greater the energy transferred. So what makes the faster wave motion and greater energy transferred from electrons in atoms or in antennas.

All Energy Transmission by Photons

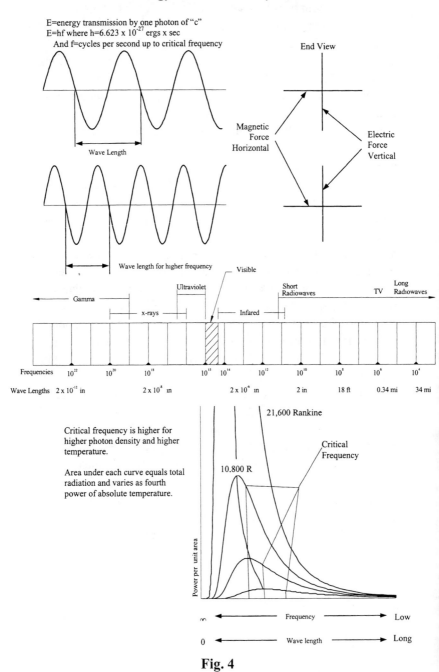

Fig. 4

Photon Energy Source

Scientists believe that atoms are such that the energy of the electrons orbiting the nucleus is greater as their distance from the nucleus is greater. They believe the electrons vibrate at an increasing frequency as their distance from the nucleus increases and that this frequency is a whole number per orbit. They also believe that the electrons spin around their own axis as they do all of the above. Then when an electron emits one photon, its distance from the nucleus is reduced from where it had more energy and a higher frequency to where it has less energy and a lower frequency. This change will determine the frequency of the photon. This change will be in various fixed amounts depending on various fixed allowed changes in the electron's distance from the nucleus.

This is only true for electrons in atoms emitting visible light or higher frequencies. Visible light means that the photon can be seen. Watch out now. This photon is invisible until it hits the retina of our eye. Then and only then is a photon visible. We can not see where a photon came from or how far away it was when it was emitted or reflected. We only see it after it is absorbed in our retina. How then, can we judge distance? We will discuss that later.

Now we can say that the different frequencies of the visible light which are absorbed by the retina of our eye will look to a brain like different colors. The range or various frequencies of these colors is called a spectrum. When the elements of the Periodic Chart are heated to incandescence, their photons are visible and make characteristic spectra or light bands which reveal their structure. This is done with a spectrometer so the frequency of the bands of the spectra can be determined.

However, if the retina is presented with visible photons of a large number of light frequencies at once, the color will be what is called white. If the retina is presented with photons of frequencies above blue in the ultra violet, they will appear invisible. Likewise those photon frequencies below red in the infra red are invisible.

Now we should remember that the higher the frequency the more energy or heat a photon can transfer but one photon comes from one electron in one atom or a free electron in motion. Energy

41

or heat is transferred from electrons in all the atoms or from free electrons within a substance or from the surface of a substance. So let's consider a square inch of the surface of a substance so we can determine the amount of energy or heat transferred per unit of time from that square inch. That will be like the density of photons or the number per second per square inch. Well, we can't count the photons but we can measure the temperature of the square inch and we can measure the amount of energy or heat the square inch puts out per second! We can do that with photons of all different frequencies even though our square inch stays the same temperature but the density changes. And what do you think we will find the energy or heat output per square inch at a constant temperature to be when we increase the photon frequency? That's right, it goes up as the frequency increases but only to a limiting frequency and then it goes down again to zero, see curves on Fig. 4. The limiting frequency is a little higher for higher temperatures but of course we can't have an infinite frequency so it seems as though there must be a limiting high temperature like a limiting photon density or the zero absolute temperature and the limiting velocity of photons. What do you think? What this really says is that as photons frequency increases the photons can travel closer together from the same emission temperature.

The reason for the photon frequency limit involves quantum mechanics which we will not tempt you to understand.

Photon Emission, Reflection, Transparency, and Polarization

Up until now we have talked about emitted and absorbed photons but most of the photons we see are reflected light photons. The only light photon emission sources other than the sun are from heat as in oxidation or fire, the moving electron heated wire of a light bulb, light from a fluorescent material excited by electrons or a gas ionized by electrons or an electrically excited laser. Most of these sources are reflected by the surface of their glass containers and again by your surroundings before they enter your retina. Besides reflecting, light photons go right through transparent material like gases, water and many liquids and material, like glass, silicon, diamond and other rocks. Instead of wondering why light photons go through transparent material, you might wonder why light photons don't go through all materials. There is certainly plenty of room in atoms for light photons to get through. As a matter of fact, the photons can go through all materials if they are thin enough. Say only a few atoms think.

The reason light photons don't go through most materials is that they run into electrons because the electrons are arranged in various patterns by the various crystal formations of their atoms. These crystal formations are duplicates over and over so that open paths for photons are evidently not available. Glass is considered a super cooled fluid and has no crystallizing structure.

Light photons which are transmitted through transparent material slow down because the velocity of photons through transparent material is less than through a vacuum. When they slow down, the change in velocity causes the wave front to change direction on entering or leaving the material surface at an angle other than 90 degrees. (See Fig. 5) If they enter the material at an angle this change in direction is called refraction and is the basis upon which microscopes, telescopes, and eyeglasses are designed.

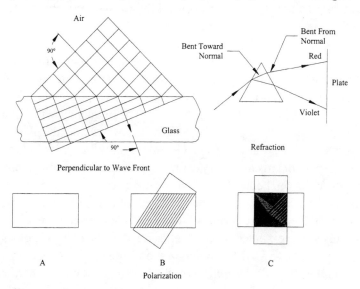

Fig. 5

The transparent materials can be such that the electromagnetic force waves shown on Fig. 5 can penetrate in only one plane. These transparent materials produce plane polarizing material. If light passes through a sheet of tourmaline such that the electric waves are vertical and the magnetic waves are horizontal, then these photons will not pass through another sheet of tourmaline turned 90 degrees or at a right angle to the first sheet of tourmaline. However, if the second sheet is held at 45 degrees to the first sheet about half the photons will get through. This is shown as A, B, and C on the chart. Polarization of light demonstrates that the photon waves are transverse waves and not longitudinal waves as are sound waves.

Otherwise, the photons are either absorbed or reflected. Reflection can keep all the photons in the same order and at the same angle to the vertical if they impinge on a polished metal surface which is smoother than the wave length of the photons. It is called a mirror. If the surface is not smooth the reflected photons will leave at various angles and only light will be reflected, not a mirror image. The high degree of reflections of metal is thought to be possible because of the abundance of free electrons in metal which readily respond to photons of light wave frequency. The reflection of ultra violet, red and radio photons from metal does not require a very smooth surface. In any case, the impingement of photons on a surface must either reflect the energy or raise the temperature or both. To reflect, a photon must react with an electron. There is nothing else to react with except a nucleus and it's doubtful that a photon of visible light frequency will have much reaction with a proton or a neutron. Now whether the photon which impinges on a surface electron simply bounces off the electron or imparts its energy to the electron and the electron emits another photon, I don't know , but it can make a difference. In the case of the sun shining on the green leaf of a tree or a red brick; either all the light frequency photons are absorbed and green and red photons are emitted or only the green and red frequency photons are reflected and all the others are absorbed. You must also remember that all the other non visible frequency photons are either absorbed, reflected or go right through the leaf and the brick.

We have talked about transparency and reflection of light

photons but lower frequency photons like radio go right through most material as do very high frequency X-ray photons and most materials includes us. Very low frequency photons go right through the earth. Radio photons are reflected from a sphere of ions which surrounds the earth. However, they must approach the ionosphere at a relatively shallow angle or they will go right through and on out into space.

Let's think for a minute of all the photons of all the frequencies which are flying all around us in all directions, through us and within us at all times. Think for one thing about their speed. I know you realize they go 186,000 miles a second, but how fast is that? Do you realize that if you light a match, the light photons could go seven times around the earth before you could blow it out in one second. That's fast.

Most of the photon radiation about us and through us is reflected. Any absorption and emission are balanced. If we don't reflect, our temperature increases. On the other hand, if we go out on a cold night, we emit photons much faster than we absorb them and we must burn food much faster than normal to keep our temperature constant. In the same way the earth would emit all the earth's heat into outer space if it were not for the sun. The sun radiation plus the earth's core heat just about balance what the earth radiates into outer space so the earth stays essentially the same temperature.

The photon radiation from the sun to the earth not only keeps us warm, it also pushes us away a little against gravity. If a photon impinges on a surface it exerts a force. If it is reflected, the force is twice as great; once when it strikes and once again when it is pushed away. This is only true if the surface does not increase in temperature. An impinging photon is a massless force and exerts a force as though it were a mass. This force per unit of area per unit of time is expressed as 1,350 watts per square meter which when divided by the photon velocity and converted to force equals 4.5×10^6 newtons per square meter. If we change newtons to .2248 pounds each and multiply times the square meters of the earth which the sun pushes on we get 1.012×10^{-6} pounds per square meter times 128.68×10^{12} square meters which is 130.22×10^6 pounds or 130,220,000 pounds. That is not much compared to the sun's gravity force on the earth at 132×10^{23} pounds.

Chapter 7
All About Liquid and Gas

Atomic Bonding and Change of State by Latent Heat

Now that we have considered the radiant force of the sun on the earth and the ability of the photon force to transfer energy or heat from electron to electron, we should be ready to consider the forces of atomic bonding which create molecules and crystals in solids. First, we must again refer to the Periodic Chart of the atoms and notice that each of the seven periods start with atoms which have only one electron in the outer shell. This means that very little force is required for that lone electron to be acquired by another atom which may have six or seven electrons in its outer shell and would like to acquire another. If this happens, the first atom in the period would have eight electrons in its outer shell even though it become an ion and the other atom is closer to eight electrons in its outer shell even though it becomes an ion. Atoms seem to prefer making molecules where they end up with eight electrons in their outer shell even though they become ions. Eight electrons in an outer shell represents stability as in the noble gases. So, as we progress across a period the less likely atoms are to loose an electron to become a molecule but the more likely they are to gain one as they have six or seven electrons in the outer shell. Then when an atom has eight electrons in this outer shell it is completely satisfied and has no desire to gain or lose an electron. The atoms are rated across a period by their increase in ionization potential which gets higher and higher as their ability to hold on to their valence electrons increases. Ionization potential is an atom's holding force for their valence electrons. As an atom's ionization potential becomes high, so does its ability to gain an electron become high. In other words, an atom can not readily hang on to one, two, or three valence electrons but it will not release any of five, six, or seven valence electrons. So, when atoms with only a few valence electrons become molecules they generally give up electrons and become ions, but atoms with many valence electrons may share electrons but they will never become ions with fewer electrons.

So ideally, atoms chemically bond into molecules when they can all end up with eight electrons in their outer shell even though they are ions. But atoms may bond into molecules without electron transfer and without ionization. For instance all the gas elements except the noble gases fly around as two atom molecules. Both the oxygen and nitrogen which make up our air are two atom molecules and oxygen has six valence electrons and nitrogen has five. There is no way these two gases would give up an electron but they are willing to share until a better deal comes along. If they receive enough photon energy and reach a high enough temperature, they will separate into atoms again.

Now that we have atoms bonded into molecules, we should consider molecules bonded into substances. Substances, like atoms, come in three states, solid, liquid, and gas and the bonding of the atoms or molecules into each state is quite different. As we said, all the elements except helium will go from a solid to a liquid to gas from absolute zero temperature to as high a temperature as it takes. However, some elements go directly from a solid to a gas under some conditions. This is called sublimation. Now if the elements will do that so will the molecules of these elements.

When atoms or molecules of a substance change from a solid state to a liquid state, the change from the kind of bond they have in the solid state to the kind of bond they have in the liquid state requires energy. This energy comes from the excess of photons the substance receives over those which it emits. As this energy is supplied to the solid, its temperature rises to a certain value called the fusion temperature. At this temperature, the electron's motion no longer increases so the temperature stays constant until all of the atom or molecule solid state bonds are released and the atoms or molecules will now slide around each other with no crystal bond.

So what is the difference in the solid state and liquid bonds. Well, the solid state bonds are such that the atoms or molecules are arranged in various configurations of crystals shown on the Periodic Chart of the atoms. The liquid atoms or molecules are not so arranged and will slide around each other with a bond still strong enough to keep the liquid from being a gas. This bond allows atoms or molecules to evaporate or condense from the surface at any temperature up to boiling temperature and pressure.

Now we should review those forces which are the same as those which keep atoms from touching-remember? Fig. 6 shows the bonding force attracting atoms together even though their electrons repel each other while their nuclei attract each other's electrons as well as there own. So you can see that the crystal bond force can be substantial and take quite a high force on the atoms to break while the Vander Waals force takes less force to break the bond. This chart shows again the tremendous force available to prevent atomic touching. When gas atoms or molecules are said to be impacting each other and an inclosure wall with perfect elasticity such that their bounce is as fast as their hit, you can see why. They never really hit. The distance "d" never really goes to zero. Remember, atoms have nothing to hit each other with except electrons and their electrons are much more powerful than you think.

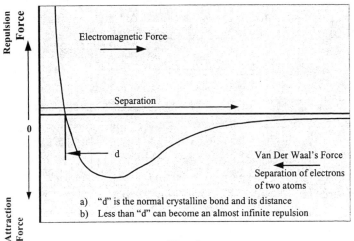

Fig. 6

So the energy required to break this crystal bond when changing state from solid to liquid is called the latent heat. Latent means hidden since the temperature doesn't rise while the bonds are broken. When a fluid looses heat and changes into a solid again, the latent heat is given up at a constant temperature again until the bonds are formed and the atoms are locked in their crystals as a solid. Then as photons are emitted faster than absorbed, the electron motion decreases and so does the temperature.

Again when the state changes from a solid to a liquid, the liquid atoms or molecules move with respect to each other and diffuse in each others space so that the liquid eventually all reaches the same temperature provided the photon emission and absorption are balanced. When boiling occurs and the state changes from a liquid to a gas at a constant temperature, the energy required to break the liquid bond is also called the latent heat and when the gas again condenses to a liquid this latent heat is given up at a constant temperature as the liquid bond again forms. The liquid state bond requires much more energy to break than the solid state bond. The liquid bond has to do with what is called the Van der Waals force which creates liquid surface tension and makes possible the meniscus on a glass of water but not all liquids. Always the liquid atoms or molecules on the surface are drawn back down under the surface since there are no liquid atoms or molecules above the surface to attract them up. This tends to create a surface tension force which makes drops of water spherical for instance. For evaporation to take place, atoms or molecules must have a high enough velocity toward the surface to break through the surface tension.

Gas Laws and Avogadro

Remember there is just about as much empty space in a liquid or gas atom as there is in a solid atom. Remember also the solid, liquid, and gas states have only to do with the atom and molecule bonds not how much space there is in the atoms. In the solid and liquid state the nuclei stay about the same distance apart. In the gas state, the distance between the atoms or nuclei changes drastically depending on the gas temperature and pressure. The

49

gas pressure depends upon the volume of an enclosure which must be used to keep the gas from drifting completely away and mixing with what ever is in the surrounding space like air.

In an enclosure the gas atoms or molecules will move about impacting each other and the inside of the enclosure creating a force on the inside of the enclosure. The amount of this force on each unit of area (say one square inch) is called the gas pressure. If the gas atoms or molecules receive more photons than they emit, their electrons will move faster which makes them rebound faster when they impact each other so they will create a higher temperature, a greater force on the inside of the enclosure and therefore a higher pressure which is force per unit area.

If the inside volume of the enclosure is reduced, the gas atoms or molecules will be closer together so they don't move as far before they impact. The greater number of impacts per unit of time on the inside of the enclosure will create a greater force and therefore a greater pressure. Since the greater number of impacts per unit of time will cause the electrons to move faster, the temperature will increase as well as the pressure. However, this increase in temperature will cause the enclosure to emit more photons than it absorbs so the temperature will decrease until the emission and absorption of photons by the enclosure is balanced.

With this background scientists have found that there is a relationship between the volume, the absolute temperature and the pressure on the gas enclosure walls which they have called the general gas law. It goes like this:
$$\frac{P_1 V_1}{T_1} = \frac{P_2 V_2}{T_2}$$

Here again we have forces moving mass through space in time. The forces are the electron repulsion forces, which cause the gas atoms or molecules, which are the mass, to impact each other and move away at the same velocity. The velocity, which is the mass motion through space in time is measured by the gas temperature and pressure which is determined by their volume or the size of the space through which each atom or molecule moves between impacts. So if you know the pressure, volume and absolute temperature of a gas, you can call them P_1, V_1 and T_1. Then you can multiply P_1 times V_1 and divide by T_1 and get a number. Then if you change any of the P_1, V_1, or T_1 values, you know that either or both of the other two have to change so that P_2 times V_2 divided by T_2 have to equal the same number you got before. You don't have to do this but it is interesting to know that you could if you wanted to and it would always work provided P, V and T were within the values readily available on earth and the substance remained a gas.

Gas Laws to Heat and Cool

Whenever we think about gas, we should think about Avogadro, an Italian count from long ago who decided that all gases at the same temperature and pressure have the same number of atoms or molecules in a given volume. Since no one could count the atoms or molecules, no one believed him. Long after Avogadro died, scientists were able to tell the atomic or molecular weight of various gases and this is how they did it. Remember in the *Periodic Table of the Elements*, each element has an atomic number and an atomic weight. The atomic number is the number of protons in the nucleus which is the same as the number of electrons. The atomic weight is the total number of protons and neutrons in the nucleus. This number represents the weight of a particular element compared to all the other elements. An atom of oxygen has an atomic weight of 16 compared to 12 for carbon, so an atom of oxygen is 16/12 times as heavy as an atom of carbon. The molecular weight of CO_2 is 12 for carbon and 32 for two oxygen which is 44 for CO_2 or carbon dioxide. So now scientists could weigh given volumes of various gases and find out if the weights at the same temperature and pressure were proportional to their atomic or molecular weights. They were and still are. That is not really amazing but it's interesting. Now scientists have a number they call Avogadro's number although Avogadro had nothing to do with his number. This number is 6×10^{23} and is the number of atoms or molecules in 12 grams of carbon 12 or of 22.4 liters of any gas at standard temperature and pressure which is 0 degrees centigrade and 760 millimeters of Mercury. This is about 32 degrees F and 15 lbs. per square inch. This is just in case you're still interested.

As an example of the use of the natural gas laws we have

discussed we will consider an air conditioner and a refrigerator. One cools the air in a house and the other freezes water into ice and cools the air in a refrigerator. Here we use the gas laws and the latent heat of condensation and vaporization laws. They apply in a very simple manner. In both cases a fixed amount of what is called a refrigerant or Fluorocarbon is used. There are many variations of Fluorocarbon depending on the temperature change desired.

Air Conditioner Section Sketch

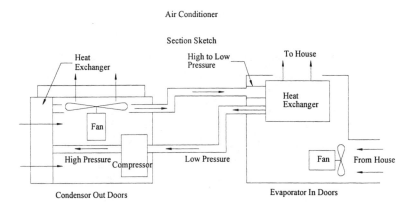

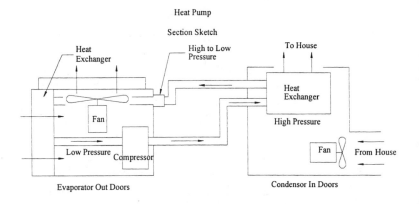

Fig. 7

For either air conditioning or refrigeration, the key element is an electric motor driven compressor which raises the refrigerant gas pressure from about 40 lbs. per in.^{2} to about 140 lbs. per in.^{2} for an air conditioner and from about 25 lbs. per in.^{2} to about 250 lbs. per in.^{2} for a refrigerator. To show how this works for an air conditioner see sketch Fig. 7. Here you will see the compressor located within the condenser which is located out of doors. The compressed refrigerant from the compressor is fed into a condenser through tubing. The condenser tubing is formed into a heat transfer unit where out door air is blown over it until the high pressure refrigerant cools enough to condense into a liquid.

The liquid refrigerant now flows through the tube into the house where it goes through an expansion unit which increases the volume and reduces the pressure to a low value so that it immediately turns into a cold gas in the evaporator. Here the drop in temperature because of both the latent heat of evaporation and expansion in accordance with the gas law $\dfrac{P_1 V_1}{T_1} = \dfrac{P_2 V_2}{T_2}$

reduce the temperature of the refrigerant gas to about 40^0 F. Therefore as the air from the house is blown through the evaporator it is cooled to a temperature below the out door temperature. This cooling of the indoor air heats the refrigerant gas which now flows through a tube back to the condenser. However, the refrigerant is still much cooler than the indoor or outdoor air, therefore the tube which returns the refrigerant to the compressor must be insulated to prevent condensation and temperature change.

The cycle for a refrigerator is just about the same except for a little difference in refrigerant and the difference in the compressor inlet and outlet pressures necessary to get down to ice making temperature of about -10^0 F. For a refrigerator, all the heat removed is dumped in the house instead of outside. The condenser is generally in back of or beneath the refrigerator.

When the same units are used as a heat pump to warm instead of cool a house, the hot high pressure as from the compressor is run into the inside heat transfer unit where it is cooled by heating the house. Then it is expanded and further cooled before it goes to the outside coils where the outside air heats it even though the outside air is colder than the inside air. If the outside air is too cold, electric heat must be added to the inside air.

L. W. WIGHTMAN

Atmosphere and Water

One of the strangest and most prevalent gases on earth is water vapor or steam which is the gas of the liquid water which covers two thirds of the earth. Water is a molecule of two gases hydrogen and oxygen. Oxygen is one of the two gases which makes up the air we breath. Nitrogen, which makes up 80 percent of the air, is essentially inert. The others are carbon dioxide, argon, neon, hydrogen, helium, etc. These two gases we share with all the plants on earth. We use oxygen and exhale carbon dioxide and plants use carbon dioxide and put out mostly oxygen. It looks like this:

Respiration (breathing) $C_6H_{12}O_6 + 6O_2 \rightarrow 6CO_2 + 6H_2O$
Photosynthesis (plants) $6CO_2 + 6H_2O \rightarrow C_6H_{12}O_6 + 6O_2$

We could not live so well without each other and you should always remember that, if nothing else. The livable part of the earth's atmosphere is like the solid part of an atom, almost not there. Contrary to what you might think, if the earth were the size of a two foot diameter globe, the livable atmosphere would be .0072 inches thick or 25,000 feet. That is less than twice the thickness of a piece of news paper. So breath away while you can.

The water in the ocean does what is called evaporation. This means that water molecules of H_2O jump off of the surface of this liquid H_2O and become H_2O water vapor. The H_2O means that each molecule has two hydrogen atoms and one oxygen atom. Some of the water vapor bounces off air molecules and goes back into the ocean where it is forced below the surface because the bonding force on water surface molecules tends to pull them beneath the surface. However, more molecules move fast enough to break through the surface attraction and jump out than bounce back in. So water vapor forms above the surface of the ocean and is called humidity. If enough water vapor forms, the water vapor molecules will bounce back into the ocean as fast as they jump out and the atmosphere will have 100 percent humidity. This doesn't often happen unless the temperature decreases because the evaporation process is about proportional to the absolute temperature. If the temperature rises the water vapor will rise high above the ocean until the temperature decreases at high altitude

54

where the water vapor will condense into tiny drops of water around bits of dust and become a cloud. Then hopefully the cloud will blow over some land and the temperature will decrease so that the tiny drops become raindrops large enough for gravity to cause them to fall on the land and grow plants to make oxygen so we can breath.

As we go high above the clouds in the atmosphere where airplanes fly, the air gets less and less dense and colder and colder until it is about minus 100 degrees Fahrenheit at about 10 miles high. Then we enter the stratosphere where the thinner air begins to get warmer until we get to about 31 miles high and a temperature of about freezing or 32 degrees Fahrenheit. Above this is the mesosphere where the temperature goes down to about minus 150 degrees Fahrenheit at about 62 miles. From here up, the temperature gets hotter in the thermosphere until it is about 980 degrees Fahrenheit at about 125 miles up where the astronauts orbit. Of course, this is in the sunlight and there are not many molecules to be found at this temperature. In the shade, they soon get cold. So when astronauts are in the sun, their suits must protect them from the heat and not the cold.

Now that we have made clouds and rain we ought to think a little about icebergs and steam. That is the higher and lower temperature of water. When water freezes, its crystal formation causes it to expand rather than contract. Water, gallium and bismuth are the only substances which do that. When ice heats up and melts it shrinks until it gets to 39 degrees Fahrenheit then it very slowly expands. This makes the ice and the coldest water remain on the surface of oceans and all bodies of water rather than on the bottom. Only in this way can life be preserved in all bodies of water on earth. If ice formed on the bottom of all bodies of water on earth, marine life could not exist where ice existed since there would be no food. Why does water behave this way rather than like the other substance? I don't know. That is a why question, not a what or how.

Gas in a Steam Turbines and Fluid Flow

At the boiling temperature and pressure of water, all water vapor and water becomes steam. Steam is a transparent gas in which no liquid exists, it can not condense like water vapor. The gas called steam is used under high pressure to drive steam engines and turbines which in turn drive electric generators which furnish our electric power. A steam engine is considered to be a constant displacement machine consisting of one or more cylinders in which pistons reciprocate. That means the pistons go back and forth in the cylinders. High pressure steam enters the cylinder through a valve and pushes the piston out. Then the piston goes back in and pushes the steam out through a valve. Then the valve is closed and the steam pushes the piston out again. As the piston goes in and out, it is connected to a crankshaft by a connecting rod so it makes the crankshaft go around. The crankshaft extends through bearings at each end and at one end it is connected to an electric generator.

A steam turbine does the same job as a steam engine but in a turbine, axial flow blades are fastened to a shaft between bearings. The axial flow blades are kind of like axial flow room fan blades. In a turbine there are several rotating fans in a series with stationary straightening blades between each set of rotating blades. As the steam goes through the turbine, it turns the rotating blades and then is straightened by the stationary blades. You should go to a power generating station and look at one.

We have talked about liquid and gas in general so now we should think about them the way you normally think of them as the water, oil, air and gas which flows in pipes. They are all called fluids because they all flow quite a bit alike except that the gases are compressible and the liquids are not. The force which makes the fluids flow through the pipes is expressed as force per unit area or pressure. For gas, we should start with the pressure of the air at the surface of the earth where the weight of the air is .075 pounds per cubic foot. That would be .075 lbs./ft^3. As we go away from the earth or at higher altitude the weight of the air or atmosphere gets less and less. If we weigh a column of air one square inch in cross section and as high as it goes above the earth it will weigh about 15 pounds. So atmospheric pressure is 15 lbs/

in². Another weight that's nice to know is water weighs 62.4 pounds per cubic foot or 62.4 lbs/ft³.

To make these fluids flow, some kind of pressure generating machine must be used. There are many kinds of such machines depending on how much pressure is required. For high pressure, constant displacement, piston, valve or gear pumps can be used and for lower pressure, centrifugal or axial flow pumps can be used. All this says is that there are many ways to generate fluid pressure.

Gases don't generally require a lot of pressure to make them flow but they generally flow through larger diameter pipes. Because of the lower pressure, gas pressure is generally measured in inches of water called head or H. The flow is generally measured in cubic feet per minute called Q or C.F.M. Since the atmospheric pressure is equal to a head of 32 feet of water, a head of inches of water does not cause much change in gas volume because of pressure. Therefore the flow of gas Q is generally considered to be the average velocity through a pipe times the cross sectional area of the pipe or Q=VA and the velocity is considered to be V= 4000√H ft per minute where H equals the difference in head from upstream someplace to downstream someplace and √H is the square root of H. Therefore, Q=4000A√HC.F.M. However, to get an accurate measure of flow, coefficients must be used for changes in pipe size, curves etc. Coefficients are corrections based on tests. Therefore, this whole business becomes a matter of experience and testing. The flow of heating gas is generally through smaller pipes at higher pressure and the flow is measured at the outlet by a meter. The same is true of drinking water furnished to homes. Both water pressure and gas head have two measurements. If the measuring tube is pointed directly into a stream it measures the total pressure or total head in inches of water. If the measuring tube is pointed directly into the stream but is closed on the end with in hole on the side of the tube, it measures the static pressure or static head in inches of water. The velocity pressure then equals the total pressure minus the static pressure. With the pressures and the measurements of the cross sections areas, bends and coefficients the flow and velocity can be found in various parts of a fluid flow path. It's nice to know that.

Lubrications

One of the most important applications of a knowledge of fluid flow in combination with fluid characteristics is in the lubrication of bearings with oil. The main reason oil is the favored material for lubrication is its high molecular attraction for metals and most material surfaces as well as its intermolecular resistance called viscosity. Rather than surface attraction of itself like water, oil will creep along a surface as long as it has molecules to supply the creep. A sharp edge will slow the creep some. This force which determines whether liquid molecules are attracted more to their own molecules or to the molecules of a solid surface is called its capillary attraction. If oil is in contact with a metallic vertical surface, its molecules will creep up the surface against the force of gravity. It will climb through a small hole in a tube or between two surfaces close together. This is called capillary attraction. It will cause the oil to fill the space between a bearing and the shaft. Therefore, as the shaft turns the oil is carried between the shaft and the bearing under the loaded part of the bearing. The only way the oil can get out is through the ends of the bearing and that path is so long and narrow that a lot of pressure is required for the oil to flow out the ends because of its viscosity. That is the pressure which supports the load so the shaft does not touch the bearing. That is the only way rotary motion of machines is maintained over long periods of time. So if bearings are kept lubricated to make up for the creep, most machines will last forever or there about.

You may wonder how the oil gets into the unloaded part of the bearing. There are several ways. It may be forced to go through a hole in the unloaded side of the bearing or through the bearing itself if it is porous as some bearings are. It may go through the end of the bearings because of a spiral groove in the shaft. But in any case oil likes to be in the unloaded part of the bearing because of capillary attraction.

Metals

The crystals that form when liquid substances freeze and become solids give the solids a large variation in characteristics such as; hardness, strength and ductility at various temperatures. Many of the metals can be mixed together to form mixtures called alloys which are harder or stronger or more ductile than any of the elements from which they are alloyed. Some of these alloys are drawn into wire to hold up bridges or make music or carry electricity. Drawing is a process where an alloy or metal rod is pulled through many successively smaller and smaller holes called dies. This causes its crystals to become drawn out to longer and longer, finer and finer filaments of tremendous strength. Drawing is used to make copper wire but the wire must be heated to soften it between draws since its purpose is to conduct electricity, not to be strong.

Other metal alloys are made to be so strong they will machine steel and other metals. Machine means to cut. Some alloys are made to punch metal parts through dies to size and form them into washing machines and automobiles and the like

If you again look at the *Periodic Chart of the Atoms* you will notice that the metallic like elements tend to be on the beginning side of each shell expect beyond Mercury. Therefore they will more or less all conduct a flow of electrons and are called electric conductors. The elements with a high number of electrons in their outer shell will not readily conduct a flow of electrons and are therefore called electric insulators. They are not metals.

Chapter 8
We Should All Understand Electricity

Electromagnetic Forces

At the present time we all live in a society which has recently discovered the uses of electricity. Almost everyone is familiar with electricity but almost no one really has the slightest idea how it works. For instance, most educated people do not realize that electricity is nothing without magnetism. Magnetism is generally never even mentioned in connection with electricity. Most so called, educated people, know only how to screw in a bulb, push in a plug or turn on a switch. That is the height of stupidity, so don't stop here, follow me. It's really simple.

Let's ponder the simple nature of the motion of stuff because of the electromagnetic forces. Forget the nuclear forces and gravity for now. You know about the mutual attraction of protons and electrons. You know about the repulsion of protons for each other and the repulsions of electrons for each other. You know that all elements have a balance of the same number of electrons as protons. You know about valence electrons from one to eight in all the elements. You know about how elements combine and make molecules where some become ions which means they have a few more or less electrons than protons. You know about the three states, solid, liquid and gas; and you know that most all the elements can be in any of these states simply by adding or subtracting to the amount of motion and the frequency of their parts by means of photons. Isn't that simple?

Now let's talk about something else we can do with electrons. We can make electrons leave their atoms or molecules and move about through atoms, molecules or substances. Remember there is scads of room in which to move. When the electrons move about they are called electricity. Now a magnetic force will make the electrons move but when they move they always generate a magnetic force which in turn can move electrons which in turn generates a magnetic force and on and on. That is why the forces are called the electromagnetic forces. However, the force we are going to use to make the electrons leave their atoms and move through a substance is not the same force which attracts the electron to its nucleus. That was an electro atomic force and this is a magnetic force. The magnetic force can cause valence electrons to leave their atom and move away. Of course other electrons will immediately take their place. In this manner, valence electrons flow through a material. The magnetic force can make them all want to flow in the same direction.

Electron Flow vs Electric Current

Now let's stop and review the scientific screw up where the electrons flow one way and scientists say the electric current flows in the opposite direction. They have a way of telling which way the current flows. It is from plus + to minus - even though the electrons go from minus to plus. They use a so called "right hand" rule based on this plus to minus current direction. In fact, all standard electrical markings and instructions used by electricians are based on this backwards plus to minus current direction. So always keep this in mind.

Lightning, Batteries, and Generators

So, how do we get a force to make the electrons move. Well I'd say there are three ways. The first is a natural way. You wait for a storm and watch the electrons jump from cloud, to cloud, from a cloud to the ground or from the ground to a cloud. From wherever there are too many electrons to wherever there are too few. This same kind of electron motion takes place on the surface of some materials so that electrons will leave the surface of one material and collect on the surface of poor electron conductors called insulators when they are rubbed together. These surface electrons are called static electrons. For that reason the electrons don't move through the insulator and disburse as they would on a good electron conductor. The good conductors are metals with silver, copper, gold and aluminum in that order the best conductors. If you were to look at the periodic table you would see that the valence electrons for silver are farther form the nucleus than those for copper and those for gold are farther from the nucleus than those for silver. What works for silver does not work for gold. It seems reasonable that the further the valence electrons are from the nucleus, the easier they can be moved away from the nucleus. This is not the case.

The second way to get a force to make electrons move is chemical. The chemical electron movers are called batteries. Batteries are made in two general categories, dry cells and wet cell, or storage batteries. The dry cells have their liquid electrolyte held in an absorbent material. They are not rechargeable. The storage batteries use a liquid electrolyte and are rechargeable. Liquid electrolytes have chemical names such as acids, bases, and salts. In all cases an ion reaction in the electrolyte releases electrons which are available on one electrode and it causes a lack of electrons on the other electrode. In the storage battery each electrode is connected to a series of metallic plates and the plates alternate positions in the electrolyte. The metallic plates must be of different metals. The lead acid storage batteries are the most common kind. The plates are lead peroxide and lead or lead antimony. The electrolyte is a sulfuric acid H_2SO_4 solution. Each molecule is composed of two hydrogen atoms, one sulfur atom and four oxygen atoms. This solution becomes weaker with use but if the electric current is reversed by charging, the solution is restored. A charge is an electron and charging means running an electron current. There are other variations to this description. Strangely, the electrode with extra electrons available is called the negative electrode, the other is called positive. The use of batteries to move electrons is by far the most expensive but also the most convenient way to furnish electricity for many applications.

The third way to get a force to make electrons move is mechanical. Any way to get rotary motion will do. A wind mill, a water wheel, a dam and water turbine, a coal, oil or gas burning steam boiler and steam engine or turbine, a nuclear reactor heated steam boiler and steam turbine. All these will make an electron moving generator rotate. An electric generator is a rotating machine that generates the motion of a magnetic force which makes electrons move. The motion of electrons is almost always through copper wire or cable. Silver wire conducts electrons easier but it costs too much. Aluminum costs less than copper but it doesn't conduct electrons as well and it is difficult to connect. The flow of electrons can be made to go only in one direction which is called D.C. for direct current or it can be made to alternate from forward to backward to forward again which is called A.C. for alternating current. All electric power generated in the U.S.A. is alternating current power.

For electrons to flow, they must flow through a material like a metal which readily conducts the flow of electrons. The word conductance means how easily electrons flow through a material and the word resistance means how difficult it is to make electrons flow through a material. All materials are rated for their conductance and resistance and the good conductors are called that and the high resistors are called that. Air which is 80 percent nitrogen and 20 percent oxygen, is a resistor, but like all resistors, electrons will go through it if enough static or magnetic force is applied. The force units which make electrons flow are called potential or voltage and the amount of electrons which flow through a given cross section of a conductor or anything is called current or amperage. The resistance through which the current or amperes flow is called ohms. Thus, a given number of volts will make a given number of amperes flow through a given number of ohms resistance.

Now I know you may not understand all this right off, but it's not really as complicated as it may seem at first blush so just keep right on reading whether you understand yet or not. Now, for amperes to flow, they have to have some place to go to. They can't just spill out the end of a wire because air is such a high resistor. Therefore, electrons can only be made to flow in what is called a circuit (from circle), only it doesn't have to be a circle. A circuit can go around and around in a generator then through a transformer, and on through to your neighborhood, through another couple of transformers, then into your house and through your appliances, then out of your house through the transformers and all the way back to the generator. If at any place along this journey the circuit is broken, the electrons will stop flowing and the voltage which made the electrons flow will be across the place where the circuit is broken. Therefore, this is a dangerous place. Now the transformers we mentioned in the circuit are devices for changing the voltage of the circuit above the ground voltage which is always zero. Since this circuit has transformers, it is an alternating current circuit so the electrons flow both ways alternately.

The number of amperes which flow through a particular conductor at a particular temperature for a given voltage is called the conductance which depends on the resistance of the conductor material. These values are established so that one volt will cause one ampere to flow through a conductor of one ohm resistance. All elements have a different resistance. The resistance of most metallic conductors will vary directly with the absolute temperature of the conductor through the normal temperature range in which we exist. This proportionality stops at very high temperature and close to absolute zero.

There are some materials called semiconductors which have a non linear proportionality between the voltage and current. The resistivity decreases with increased temperature for silicon and germanium with certain impurities.

There are other materials called superconductors whose resistance goes to zero at temperatures about seven degrees Rankine. These are common metals like aluminum, tin, lead, zinc and indium. More recently superconductor materials have been developed with zero resistance above 180 degrees Rankine.

When electric current is induced in rings of superconducting material, it flows forever since the resistance is zero as long as the low temperature is maintained. Under these conditions a very strong magnetic force can be developed by the circulating electric current. Many applications of this technology are in the process of being developed. However, for now we will get back to our normal temperature condition.

To understand how the generator makes the electrons flow we must understand that as the electrons flow along a wire, they create a magnetic force around and around the wire. When the electrons stop the magnetic force stops. The magnetic force around a wire, through which electrons are flowing, is in a circular direction around the wire that the fingers of the right hand would take if the thumb were in the direction of the electric current which is opposite to the direction of electron flow. Remember I told you that electrical terms are such that electric current is said to flow in the opposite direction from that of the electron flow.

The magnetic force, like the other forces, is invisible and we wouldn't know it was there if we couldn't measure what it does. It is said to flow in a circuit. That is, it produces a force all the way around the circuit. However, the force cannot be felt except by the electrons and atoms in certain substances and by electrons in conductors. The substances are called ferromagnetic and are iron and iron alloys with silicon, cobalt, nickel, manganese and bismuth. A very magnetic material is alnico, an alloy, and some alloys of lanthanum, samarium, and perhaps some other rare earth metals. However iron is the basic metal which makes our use of electricity possible because of its very high conductance of magnetic force. The direction of magnetic force is said to be from south to north inside the earth and from the north to the south outside the earth. Outside the earth the magnetic force is called the magnetic field. However, the magnetic field doesn't push north any more than south, it simply turns the north end of an iron bar magnet south and it turns the south end north. It simply lines the bar up with the earth's flux which goes from the north to the south outside the earth. The bar doesn't go anywhere. We wouldn't know which end was which if we didn't try it out.

A strange thing about magnetic force is that if an iron bar is hardened and then magnetized, it will retain its magnetic force capability. It is then called a permanent magnet. To harden the iron bar or most any metal, it must be heated to an appreciable temperature and then cooled very rapidly by quenching. That means dipping in water or oil or the like. It is then much harder, stronger, and more brittle. If the iron bar is heated and then cooled slowly, it is said to be annealed. It is then much softer not as strong and more ductile. In this case the iron bar cannot be permanently magnetized to any extent. See flux patterns caused by current flow shown in Fig. 8.

Electromagnetic Flux Generator

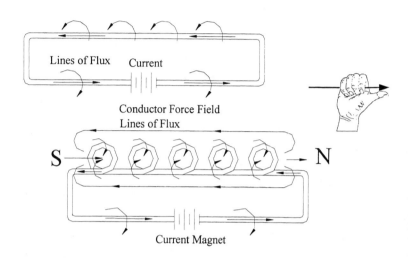

Lines of Flux   Current

Conductor Force Field
Lines of Flux

S ——————————— N

Current Magnet

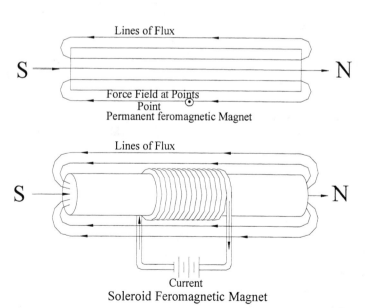

Lines of Flux

S ——————————— N

Force Field at Points
Point
Permanent feromagnetic Magnet

Lines of Flux

S ——————————— N

Current
Soleroid Feromagnetic Magnet

Fig. 8

To magnetize the iron bar, a direct current carrying insulated copper wire is wound around the bar. The amount of magnetization will be determined by the number of turns of wire wound around the bar, the length of the winding around the bar, the amount of current in the wire and the cross sectional area of the bar. To have some way to talk about the magnetic force in the bar, scientists decided to play like the magnetic force amounted to fictitious lines of force going through the bar from the south end of the bar to the north end of the bar and then back through the air to the south end of the bar. These imaginary lines of force are called lines of flux. Then the greater the magnetizing force the greater the flux density in flux lines per unit of cross section area of the bar. The flux lines of force are assumed to return through the air from the north end of the bar to the south end. Thus the magnetic flux lines all go through a magnetic circuit like electrons go through an electric circuit. The magnetic flux lines going through the air are said to create a magnetic force field. That means that at a point in the space about a magnet, there is a specific magnetic force in a specific direction. However, you can't tell the force is there until you put something at that point for the magnetic force to act upon. This magnetic force is called the magnetic field strength at that point.

Magnetic Force in Flux Field and Lenz's Rule

The magnetic force generated around a wire with a direct current of electron's flowing through it is the same force as the magnetic force in the iron bar. That magnetic force flowing in the space around the wire is the same as the magnetic field force flowing from the north end of the magnet outside back to the south end. This magnetic force at the point is in the direction of and in the amount of the density of the magnetic flux lines through the point. If we put a valence electron at this point the magnetic force does nothing to the electron. If however, the valence electron, at this point, is in a copper wire which is at a right angle to the direction of the flux lines through the point and the wire moves through the point at a right angle to the flux lines, then the valence electron will leave its atom and move along the wire providing the wire is a part of a circuit. Thus, the magnetic force moves the valence electron because of its motion at a right angle to the direction of magnetic force and its movement in a direction of a right angle to its direction before it moved. See Fig. 9 to show three right angles.

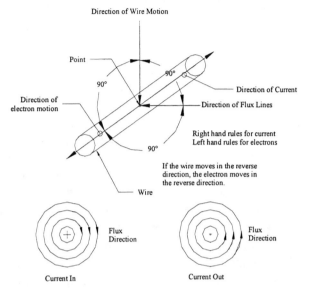

Fig. 9

This is the most important concept to understand in electromagnetics. From this we must remember that if a wire extends across a magnetic flux path, the electrons in the wire will NOT leave their atoms and move along the wire. Only if the wire MOVES across the magnetic flux path do the electrons leave their atoms and move along the wire provided the wire is part of a circuit. Now instead of moving the wire across the magnetic flux path, we can leave the wire standing still across the magnetic flux path and change the density of the magnetic flux. Then some valence electrons will leave their atoms and move along the wire. This will happen with any change in the flux density. The direction of the electron flow will be such that the magnetic flux this electron flow generates will oppose the change of the flux which caused the electrons to flow in the first place. This is called Lenz's rule. Remember it. The way Lenz's rule works is shown in Fig. 10.

How Electrons Flow in a Coil Rotating through Field Flux

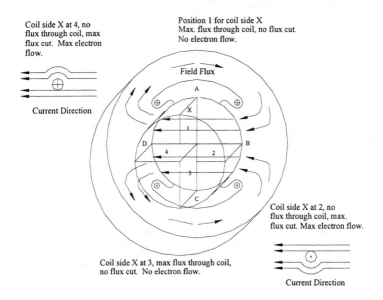

Coil side X at 4, no flux through coil, max flux cut. Max electron flow.

Current Direction

Position 1 for coil side X Max. flux through coil, no flux cut. No electron flow.

Field Flux

Coil side X at 2, no flux through coil, max. flux cut. Max electron flow.

Current Direction

Coil side X at 3, max flux through coil, no flux cut. No electron flow.

Fig. 10

Coil side X from 1 to 2, Flux cutting increasing to max, Flux through coil decreasing to zero, Electron flux increasing from cutting, Electron flow increasing to keep flux through coil from decreasing. Coil side X from 2 to 3, Flux cutting decreasing to zero, Flux through coil flux increasing to max. Electron flow decreasing from cutting, Electron flow decreasing to prevent flux from increasing. Coil side X from 3 to 4 to 1 is the same as 1 to 2 and 2 to 3 except the electrons flow in the reverse direction.

Now let's ponder the electromagnetic forces and how they work on electrons. First the electric force is the force of attraction of an electron for its nucleus and the force of repulsion of an electron for other electrons. So an electron belongs to an atom and will not leave its nucleus unless forced to by a magnetic force. This is true whether the electron is a part of a copper atom or an iron atom or any metal atom. However, once an electron is forced to leave an atom it will move away in the direction the magnetic

69

force moves it, and as long as the magnetic force moves it. It could care less whether it joins up with another copper atom or an iron atom when it stops. To an electron any old nucleus which attracts it will do. That is why the copper wire must be insulated. So if the magnetic force which moved the electron away from its atom stops, the electron will stop and join any attractive nucleus handy. In other words, the magnetic force which moved the electron had to be great enough to overcome its electric force of attraction for all the nuclei the electron passed while the magnetic force moved it. The electron went by all the nuclei at a velocity depending on how great the force was and it kept moving as long as the force moved it.

The commonly used force which can move electrons away from their nucleus is a magnetic force which moves the electrons in the manner and direction we have just described. The magnetic force does not move all the electrons away from their nucleus, it moves only the outer electrons which are farthest from their nucleus and therefore attracted the least. The magnetic force not only moves the electrons, it lines up their axis of spin in the direction of their motion. As these electrons move along a conductor with all their spin axes lined up, they generate a magnetic force in a peripheral direction around the conductor in the same direction as their spin. This is the source of the magnetic force we have discussed for solenoids, magnets and transformers, motors, generators etc.

While the force, which moves the electrons, acts only on the outer electrons in the atoms in the conductors within a generator, the outer electrons in the complete length of the conductor circuit respond. However, the rest of the outer electrons respond in varying degrees depending on how far they are from the generator where electrons both leave and enter simultaneously. The whole conductor circuit offers a resistance to the motion of the electrons which the magnetic force within the generator must overcome. Thus the force decreases from where the electrons leave the generator to where they enter because of the resistance to their flow by the atoms of the conductor circuit.

You may wonder how the first magnetic force or the first electron movement in a wire ever took place if each event depends on the other. Well, the answer, apparently, is in the earth where the central iron part rotates at a little different speed than the outer iron part and therefore causes some electrons to move which in turn lines up the spin of enough electrons to create an earth size magnet with the north and south poles. This earth magnet is apparently strong enough to turn some natural iron which is on or near the earth surface into weak permanent magnets. Then too, as we discussed, batteries were found to make electrons move and this electron motion through a wire circuit was found to generate a magnetic force which could readily flow through iron.

Now, what is there about flowing electrons and iron electrons that creates a magnetic force? Well, scientists believe that the magnetic force around the current carrying wire wound around an iron bar will cause the electrons in the iron atoms to line up so that the axis of their spin is in line with the magnetic flux generated by the wire coil. Thus, each electron acts as a magnet and becomes a part of the bar magnet. Maybe this is true. At least there is something different about the atomic structure of iron and a few like elements which allows them to conduct magnetic flux when none of the other elements will. You might ponder that a bit.

Chapter 9
To Make and Deliver Low Cost Electric Power

Steam Turbine Driven Electric Generator

Now we should be ready to talk more about generating electric power with an electric generator driven by a steam turbine, but first we have to get the heat or energy to make the steam. There is one basic element required to do that and that is oxygen. Oxygen will make stuff burn slowly like iron rusting or when stuff combines with oxygen we may say it oxidizes or burns or explodes like dynamite. It's just different stuff combining with oxygen at different rates, slowly to very rapidly. Some other elements will burn as sodium in chlorine, zinc with sulphur, and potassium in water. However, when oxygen combines with other elements in oxidation or burning, it acquires electrons from the other elements since oxygen has six electrons in its outer shell and will not lose electrons.

So to heat water to make steam we combine coal or oil or gas with oxygen on a grate or through jets under a boiler. We then heat the steam some more in a superheater over the same fire to increase the steam pressure. We need the high pressure because as the steam turns the turbine the steam pressure, which is force, is used up. If the pressure drops too far, the steam will condense or turn back into water and water doesn't work too well in a steam turbine. Therefore, we can run the turbine exhaust steam into a condenser which is a number of exhaust steam pipes with cold river water running over them. Then the steam condenses very quickly and in so doing reduces its pressure very quickly. This adds to the pressure difference between the superheated steam and the exhaust steam and increases the force to run the steam turbines. The efficiency is a measure of how much work the turbine can do per dollars worth of coal or gas or oil used to run the turbine.

Fig. 11 shows the schematic arrangement of all the parts of a steam boiler and a steam turbine driven alternating current generator with its exciter.

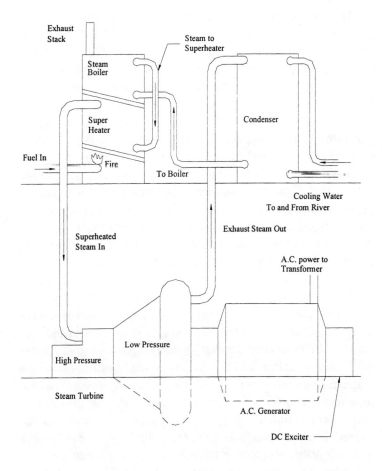

Fig. 11

WIGHTMAN

Direct and Alternating Current Generator

Now that we have a steam turbine driving an A.C. (alternating current) generator we ought to consider what makes the electricity. It's no big deal but first we have to make some D.C. (direct current) to excite the alternators rotating magnetic field. We will do this with a D.C. generator called an exciter for no good reason. The D.C. exciter is tacked on to the end of the alternator shaft opposite the drive end as shown.

In these sketches shown in Fig. 12, both the iron stationary and rotating parts are assumed to be made of soft iron laminations somewhat insulated from each other by iron oxide so that the iron electrons can not readily flow axially because of the magnetic flux flowing radially and peripherally through the iron laminations. In the D.C. exciter, the field which is the creator of the magnetic flux, is shown as arrows is the stationary part. The part which generates the D.C. output is the rotary part. In the AC generator shown in Figs. 13 and 14, the field, which is the creator of the magnetic flux, is the rotary part and the part which generates the A.C. output, is the stationary part. The reason for this is that the generator puts out a great amount of power and slip rings are not a very effective means of conducting a great amount of power. Power in this case consists of a great number of electrons going one way and then the other way in very large diameter copper conductors. Therefore, the output of the alternator must be direct from the stator winding while the field current comes from the D.C. exciter through slip rings as shown. The field and armatures coils of insulated copper electron conductors are called windings.

We must consider that as the D.C. exciter rotor rotates within a fixed stator field flux pattern so that the direction of the magnetic flux through the rotor iron constantly reverses as the rotor turns. Therefore, the commutator switches the rotor current output to one direction only, through brushes that are shown 180 degrees apart. Depending on the rotor winding this can be done in two, four, or six or more brush positions around the commutator to produce overlapping peak current outputs as shown in Fig. 15. So you see, D.C. is not a steady direct current but more of a steady by jerks current.

74

D.C. Generator Exciter

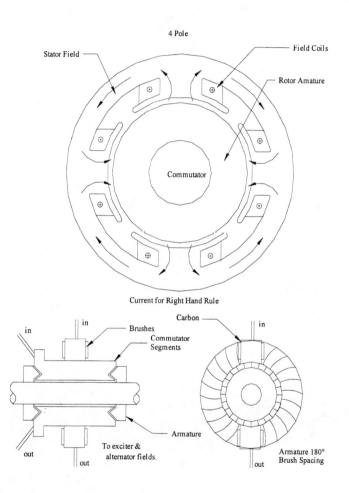

Fig. 12

75

A.C. Generator

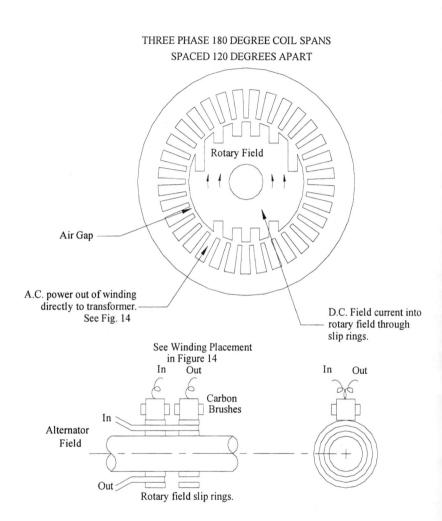

THREE PHASE 180 DEGREE COIL SPANS
SPACED 120 DEGREES APART

Rotary Field

Air Gap

A.C. power out of winding
directly to transformer.
See Fig. 14

D.C. Field current into
rotary field through
slip rings.

See Winding Placement
in Figure 14

In   Out   In   Out

Carbon
Brushes

In

Alternator
Field

Out

Rotary field slip rings.

Fig. 13

The A.C. generator rotating magnetic flux field keeps changing

The A.C. generator rotating magnetic flux field keeps changing the direction of the magnetic flux through the stator to match its position as it rotates within the stator. As the flux direction in the stator goes around with the rotor, it cuts all the stator coil windings and forces the electrons to flow in an alternating direction or right, left, right, left etc., as shown in Fig. 14.

We have talked about the generation of DC and AC electric current but, of course, the current is the result of having generated a magnetic force called volts which pushes the electrons through a copper conductor. The flow of electrons per unit of time is called current and the units of current are called amperes. If we multiply the force in volts times the current in amperes we get volt amperes or what is called watts. Watts is a measure of the rate of using energy like energy per hour. The rate of using energy is called power. Then if we multiply the watts, power times the time we have been using watts we get watt hours. Watt hours is energy. Watt hours is what we pay the electric company for, when we get a power bill, which is really an energy bill.

Three Phase 180 Degree Coil Spans
Spaced 120 Degrees Apart.

Winding Placement

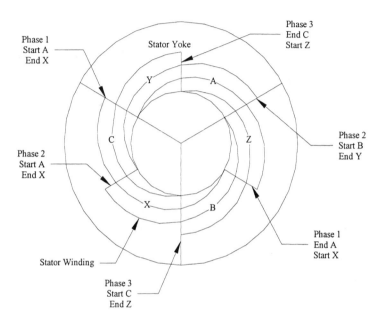

Three phases are established by three sets of two pole windings, spaced around a stator 120 degrees apart, as shown in fig. 14. Each phase is one cycle or 360 degrees or once around for the rotating field. A new phase starts each third of a rotation.

The rotating field remains two pole regardless of single phase, two phase or three phase stator winding.

One revolution of the generator creates one complete cycle of all phases. The generator runs at 3,600 revolutions per minute or 60 cycles per second.

Fig. 14

78

Now we know that the force or volts makes the current or amps, but remember we talked about how the number of amps we get for a given number of volts depends on the conductor's resistance to the flow of electrons which is called ohms. Remember we said that the voltage "E" equaled the amps "I" times the ohms. "R"

$$E = IR \quad \text{or} \quad E \text{ divided by } I = R$$

What this says is that the volts E divided by the current amps I is a constant resistance ohms R. This means that if the voltage E gets greater, the amps I must get greater to keep R constant. However, if we increase the voltage E across the resistance R to increase the current I, the increase in current I will cause the resistance R to increase in temperature. Since the resistance of metals increases with increasing temperature, R will increase so the current I will only increase to E divided by R where R is higher than before the voltage E was increased. In other words, I is proportional to E only as long as the current goes through a constant resistance R. Therefore, when we show the A.C. alternating current single phase and three phase current variation in time curves in Fig. 15, these curves would be just the same for the voltage as for the current. In fact, we might just as well call A.C. by A.V. or alternating voltage except A.C. has a precedence over A.V. and science has screwed up again because we generate an alternating voltage which always keeps time with the rotating field position and the alternating current does not except if the current is through a resistance only. Since we have agreed that the voltage E equals the current I times the resistance R and that the power W equals the voltage E times the current I or since E = IR and W = IE we can say power W = IE or

Ix IR or I^2R thus $W = I^2R$ watts.

We should note, as the drawing points out, these curves apply to power plant generation are for 60 cycle per second A.C. power output. That means that the steam turbine is driving the alternating current generator at 3600 revolutions per minute.

How Electrons Move

Direct Current

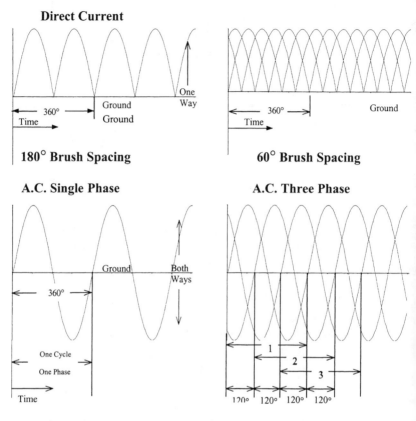

Note that for D.C. direct current, the outer electrons all travel just one way in time. For 180 degree brush spacing, the electrons go and stop, go and stop, etc. For 60 degree brush spacing, the electrons go and slow a little and go again, etc.

Note that for A.C. alternating current, the outer electrons all go one way and then stop and all go the other way and stop, etc.

For either D.C. or A.C. as the voltage is increased for electron flow in any given diameter wire or current carrier, more electrons move farther for each motion. As the number of electrons and the distance moved increases the carrier temperature increases. In some cases the carrier becomes incandescent as in a light bulb.

Fig. 15

80

Resistance, Inductance, and Capacitance

There are two conditions other than when the alternating current flow of electrons is through resistance only. Voltage current curves for these conditions are on Fig. 16. One of these conditions is called inductance and the other is called capacitance. All I'm going to tell you about them is what they are and how they work so you can know if you wish.

Inductance has to do with the energy required of the electron flow to induce the magnetic field or flux around the conductor. For instance, if the conductor is wound in a coil so that all the flux around all the turns is additive, the flux will slow the current build up in accordance with Lenz's rule so that the currents build up is behind the voltage build up as shown in the Fig. 16 for single phase. For three phase inductance the current build up will lag the voltage build up in each phase.

Capacitance has to do with the electron build up on one side of the capacitor and the electron depletion on the other side of the capacitor. A capacitor is generally made of two sheets of conducting material of the same area separated by a thin sheet of insulation. Each conducting sheet is electrically connected to one end of a current carrying conductor which is a part of a circuit. With this arrangement, the electrons, which would normally flow right and left in the conductors, can not flow through the insulator. In this case, the current build up toward the right side of the capacitor will start as soon as the voltage which forced electrons to the left begins to decrease. When it hits zero and starts forcing more electrons to the right, the current to the right is as great as it will get. As the voltage which forces electrons to the right increases, the capacitor begins to get about as many electrons on the right as it will hold so the current to the right begins to decrease. Finally when the voltage forcing electrons to the right is as high as it will get, it can't force any more electrons to the right so the current is zero. Then as the voltage begins to decrease the electrons or current start to flow back toward the left and the process repeats only backwards.

Thus, as shown in Fig. 16 we have the current in phase with the voltage for resistance only; the current trailing the voltage for inductance only and the current leading the voltage for capacitance only. If an electric circuit includes all three, resistance, inductance and capacitance; and the inductance is equal to the capitance, then the overall circuit will have current and voltage in phase. Otherwise the voltage and current will be out of phase in the direction of which ever is greater induction or capacitance. It's as simple as that.

Look at it this way. The voltage or magnetic force is generated by the position of the rotating part relative to the stationary part of an electric generator and is therefore always fixed relative to the generator rotation. However, the current or flow of electrons in the conductor circuit, which is caused by the magnetic force or voltage, is a function of the conditions of the conductor circuit. These conditions have to do with the circuit resistance, inductance, and capacitance.

Three Phase Power Transmission Through Transformers

To transmit electric power from a power plant generator to a customer over a long distance became a major problem because power stations had to be close to a source of a lot of water, which generally meant by a river or lake and customers were far from water. Therefore, as soon as the generation and use of alternating current power was worked out, the power was immediately transmitted at as high a voltage as possible. The reason was that, as we have just said, the transmission of watts of power is:

$$W = I^2 R \text{ or } IE$$

Therefore, for a given amount of power, the higher the E or volts, the lower the I or current can be. The lower the I or current can be the higher the R can be for the same power or I^2R transfer. This means that a much longer power transfer conductor with a higher resistance R can be used to transfer the same power with the lower current I.

To get to the higher voltage E, transformers were used to raise the voltage E at the power generating station and to lower the voltage back down at various locations where the power could be distributed to customers.

To show how these transformers works see Fig. 17.

Single Phase Alternating Current

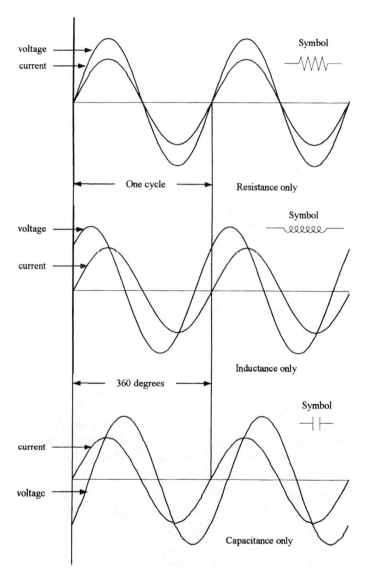

Fig. 16

Transmission

Transformers

They consist of a laminated soft core, carrying the same magnetic flux through two wound coils.

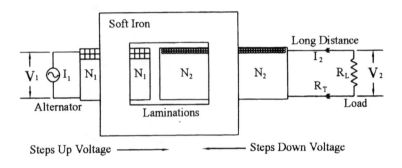

N_1 is a small number of turns of a large diameter conductor carrying a high current I_1, generated by a low voltage V_1.

N_2 is a large number of turns of a small diamter conductor carrying a low current I_2 generated by a high voltage V_2.

R_L is the load resistance.

R_T is the transmission in resistance.

The standard transformer relationship is $I_1V_1 = I_2V_2$

With a transformer the transmission loss is $I_2^2R_T$ watts, which is much lower than $I_1^2R_T$ watts.

Reverse transformer is at far end of transmission line.

Fig. 17

The drawings in Fig. 18 show what is called three phase alternating current which is the only kind of power generated in central power stations these days. The reason is that three phase power generation and transmission to your home is much less expensive than two phase or single phase. Even though it is a little tricky to visualize, all of the three phase A.C. power is carried by just the three transmission lines shown in Fig. 18. The ground carries nothing. This is possible because if you look at the three phase current output drawing, Fig 15, you will see that, at any time, the total current right is equal to the total current left. Since all of the current actually flows in the three transmission conductors, none of the current flows in the ground. The earth is considered to have no resistance in any case. You can see from the curves in Fig. 15 that when one curve is at *maximum* current, the other two are at half current running in the opposite direction. When one current is zero, the other two are equal at half current running in the opposite directions.

Of course there is a power transmission problem condition called power factor where the current lags the voltage because the overall power requirement has more inductance than capacitance which is normal. In this case the transmission efficiency decreases. If this condition gets bad enough power companies float a synchronous condenser on the line at a substation to correct the power factor. A condenser is another name for a capacitor and synchronous means it has the same phase relationship as the transmission lines.

Three phase power is often fed into factories or large power users but not into homes. Here it is split up with two phase here, two phase there and the other phase somewhere else. However, the long distance power distribution is run at very high voltage by means of transformers. This is possible because alternating current makes voltage change by transformers possible where as, it is not possible with direct current.

Transmission Systems

High voltage three phase transmission runs from about 11KV to 35KV. K means kilo or 1000 so 35KV is 35,000 volts. Three phase transmission is generally in a Y configuration.

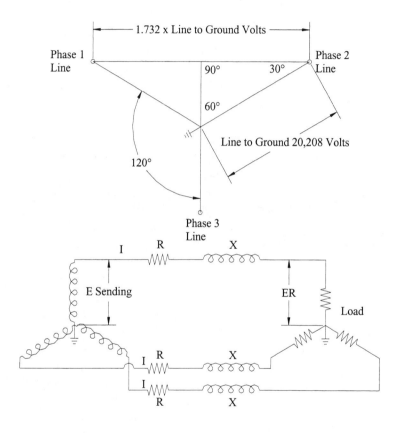

Three Phase Transmission line having resistance and reactance. Reactances x = inductance and capacitance.

Fig. 18

Power Distribution Systems
From
Three Phase Line

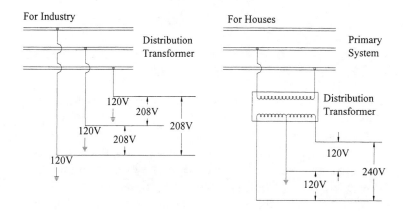

As you can see, for industry, a three phase distribution transformer brings all three phases from the three phase power line right into an operating plant. In this case the usable voltage is 208 volts from phase to phase and 120 volts from each phase to ground. This makes possible the use of three phase large horse power equipment which is more efficient than single phase equipment and requires no starting device for motors.

For houses, a single phase distribution transformer is used. You can see these on telephone poles. The output from this distribution transformer is 240 volts divided in the center into two 120 volt single phase lines. Therefore houses have both 240 volt and 120 volt single phase power available. In this case all electric motors require starting devices which make the motors think they are starting on two phase power.

Fig. 19

Chapter 10
Power Uses

Thermionic Emission

All of our discussion of electric power generation and transmission has been based on the flow of electrons though copper conductors and the flow of magnetic flux through space and iron. We have discussed the flow of electromagnetic photons through space to some extent. However, we will now discuss briefly the flow of electrons as well as photons through space.

As we know, the faster electrons move the higher the temperature. Therefore, if we apply a high enough magnetic force or voltage across a high enough metallic wire resistance, we can raise its temperature until it is red hot. Now, if we put this metallic wire in a vacuum and make it part of another electric circuit to a plate spaced a short distance from the heated wire and apply a voltage in the right direction, electrons will flow from the hot wire through the vacuum to the plate. The hotter the wire the more electrons will flow for the same voltage. If the voltage is reversed, no electrons will flow from the cold plate to the hot wire. This is called Thermionic Emission of electrons.

Photoelectric Effect and X-ray Emission

We have discussed electromagnetic forces at length and called them fields, flux, lines and waves because scientists use these terms to describe conditions these forces create with respect to electrons. Without electrons, these electric and magnetic forces don't exist. With electrons, these forces always exist. We know that photons are created by the motion of electrons and that photons are both electric and magnetic forces in a transverse wave form at the same frequently at right angles traveling at "C" velocity. We know that their combined energy is proportional to their frequency up to their critical frequency. The only source of increased energy with frequency would be the increased motion even though the "C" velocity is constant. This increased energy is demonstrated in what is called the Photoelectric Effect where photons of increasing frequency impinge on a metal surface in a vacuum. At a given frequency, generally ultraviolet, the photon energy is high enough to give an electron enough increased energy to leave the metal surface. This can be measured by picking up the electron as part of a circuit through a galvanometer. The speed of the emitted electron is increased when the photon frequency is increased. In fact, only the speed of the emitted electron is increased by the increased frequency of the photon. The only way to increase the density of the emitted electrons is to increase the density of photons, not their frequency.

Now, which of the electro magnetic photon forces do you think increases the motion of the emitted electrons, the electric or the magnetic force? Well, the only force which can move electrons for electric power generation and use is the magnetic force called volts. Therefore, I'd vote for the magnetic photon force, although I don't know how it is done.

The reverse of this electro magnetic process is the creation of x-rays by the impingement of electrons on a metal surface. Here the greater the speed of the electrons as they impact the metal surface the higher the frequency of the photons emitted. Therefore, there are a large range of very high frequency photons produced called x-rays by the impact of very high speed electrons on a metal surface. Usually the metal is tungsten but it need not be.

Photon Transmission

Now that we can make alternating current electricity, we can both vary its current and its frequency and broadcast radio information or television.

Antenna transmission and reception of photons is a straight forward electromagnetic radiation and reception. A vertical antenna can have electric signals driven up and down its length as shown in Fig. 20. As the electrons vibrate up and down the antenna, they create a magnetic field around the antenna. The vibrating magnetic field sends out a horizontally transverse magnetic wave. This vibrating magnetic field matches the vibrating vertical electric field which sends out a vertically transverse electric wave. These two waves are in phase and are electromagnetic waves or photons traveling horizontally from the vertical antenna. They tend to go parallel to the earth and follow it around at low frequency but go more in a straight line tangent to the earth at higher frequencies. The wave strength drops off about directly as the distance since they go radially and not spherically.

To receive these waves a receiving antenna must be about parallel to the sending antenna otherwise it will not be very effective. Remember the free electrons in the receiving antenna must be driven up and down at the same frequency as those in the sending antenna by nothing but the force from the energy of the photons. The sending antenna has to emit enough energy in the form of photons so that billions of receiving antennas could receive a program in order for any one of them to receive a program. The higher frequency photon waves can be received at great distances since the straight line tangent photon waves will reflect off the ionosphere which surrounds the earth..

Further, the higher frequency photons can be reflected and therefore can be focused into a beam which is aimed at a reflector on a geosynchronous, geostationary orbit satellite which is 22,238 miles above the earth's equator. This is where the earth's gravity force is equal to the centrifugal force on the satellite. These reflected photons can be received within an area of 33 percent of the earth's surface.

Electromagnetic Transmission

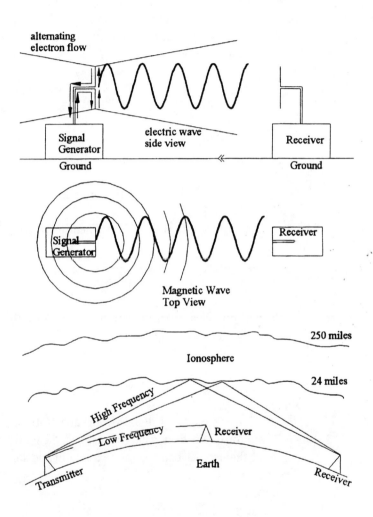

Fig. 20

General Electron Uses You Should Know About

There is nothing in your life that does not have to do with electricity or electromagnetics. The operations of your brain and all the nerves of your body are electric. Everything that involves electrons involves electricity and magnetism. Even your feelings. But while you should learn about this aspect of electromagnetics, I'm not the one to learn from because I don't know.

However, some of life's physical thing you may be familiar with will follow. Electricity from power stations is generally used in three ways.

1. Since electricity is the motion of electrons, we use this motion to create electromagnetic photon energy which we use as follows:

    a. X-ray for medical and industrial purposes.

    b. Light to see by, signal with, etc.

    c. Heat for comfort, microwave, liquid heating of all kinds.

    d. Communication by radio, TV, etc.

    e. Telescopic, and microscopic spectroscopic information.

2. Since the motion of electrons creates magnetic force, this force is used to mechanically move stuff as follows:

    a. Motors for homes, appliances, farms industry and transportation

    b. All mechanical requirements for pushing and pulling.

    c. Production of sound and signals from such motion.

3. Since the motion of electrons can be controlled, the motion of electrons themselves can be used to transmit and store information as follows:

    a. Telephone, fax

    b. Computers, calculators, information storage, etc.

Thus the three ways electromagnetism is used are (1) as the energy of photons, (2) as the force of magnetism, and (3) as the controlled movement of electrons themselves. Having said this, there is not much further we can go without getting into the design details of all the zillions of products which are based on electromagnetism and that is Engineering which you may want to consider later, especially if you are a girl.

Chapter 11
What and How of the Universe

The General Concept

To ponder what we have covered so far about the simple nature of existence which is forces moving stuff through space in time, our discussion has essentially been about the what and how of the stuff on earth. That is where we live and that should excite our greatest interest. However, like it or not, we also live in the universe and are completely dependent on what and how things happen in the universe. Our knowledge of the universe was zilch when I was born and not much greater when I graduated and went to work for General Electric. Actually, the greatest advances in the knowledge of our universe have taken place since I retired from Emerson Electric in 1979. So you will have an opportunity to be in on the cutting edge of a knowledge of our universe which is as yet almost unknown. This will be possible because we now see, not only with the limited vision of our eye, but with the frequency spectrum from radio to x-ray.

So, let's take a look at the what and how of our universe as the astronomers are finding it to be. It is certainly not like they thought it would be when they had to look at it with nothing but their eyes looking through telescopes from the surface of the earth with the atmosphere in the way.

We are starting with our sun as a star because astronomers base all star information on a comparison with our sun with a mass called Ms. This is necessary to understand what our universe consists of at present. Our universe consists of a tremendous number of stars of various sizes and ages. It also consists of an unknown number of dead stars which are invisible. It consists of a great number of stars which are dying and are still visible. It consists of places where a great number of stars are in the process of being born. All of these stars are clumped in groups called galaxies which we have discussed. However, in addition to the flat pancake type galaxies with spiral arms, there are elliptical galaxies. They do not rotate like spirals, are mostly older stars and have little gas and dust to form new stars. Then there are a few rather open galaxies which have no shape at all.

So how did the universe get this way? It could be lots of other ways and until lately everyone thought it was lots of other ways. Well, how it got this way, depends on how it evolved from the beginning in accordance with cosmologists and astronomers. Cosmologists are more interested in the whole universe or cosmos and how it got started. In the beginning there either was a previous universe or there was not a previous universe. Maybe you will find that out during your lifetime. I will not. At any rate, according to cosmologists, in the beginning there was no mass. There was, however a universe worth of radiation which is called photons which are massless energy with a motion of 186,000 miles per second called "c". They have a frequency of anything much less than infinity. The photon density also may have been anything less than infinity since astronomers figure the temperature must have been about 10^{10} Kelvin at one second 1.8 X 10^{10} Rankine. This temperature gradually cooled down until today the background radiation is about 3 degrees Kelvin or 5.4 degrees Rankine in the microwave frequency range of about 3 x 10^{11} cycles per second and a peak wave length of .079 inches.

In the meantime, much of this radiation has turned into the mass and energy we have in the universe today. Now that's been some trick and scientists have been trying to figure out how it was done for as long as there have been scientists. However, as I said, only in the last few years have scientists found some answers and here are their general concepts. Concept means what and how something might have happened.

The inflationary model of the "Big Bang" theory says that after about 10^{-35} seconds this extremely dense radiation began the process of nucleosynthesis or forming electrons and protons during expansion to a radius of 10^7 light years. That is an inflation rate of 10^{50}. The temperature dropped to about 1.8 x 10^{22} Rankine. This is faster than "c".

This process lasted for about three minutes to a temperature of 1.8 x 10⁹ Rankine after which protons, neutrons, and free electrons were available and expanding in an excess of remaining photons. However, the photons straight line flight was impeded by the free electrons which had not yet joined with the protons to make atoms. The density of mass in the universe did not exceed that of radiation for about three hundred thousand years.

After about ten thousand years had passed, expansion had cooled the temperature to about 4,000 Kelvin or 7,200 Rankine. At this time the protons and free electrons which had been formed by nucleosynthesis began to unite into neutral atoms of hydrogen and helium with a little deuterium which is hydrogen with a neutron. The helium was about 20 to 30 percent as prevalent as hydrogen. A neutral atom is one with the same number of electrons as protons. As yet no appreciable number of heavier elements existed. Since the free electrons had been used to make neutral atoms, photons began to continue in a straight line. Astronomers call this the time of decoupling of matter and radiation.

At about this time astronomers believe the uniform nature of the universe began to change and clumping into globular clusters of hydrogen and some helium began. These globulars were believed to be about 10⁵ times the mass of the sun or 10⁵ Ms. Within these globular clusters the first galaxies are believed to have formed, but when they formed is a puzzle. And why are some galaxies spirals and some elliptical? Astronomers have times and reasons for these puzzles; lots of them. Based on the red shift of the light from the expanding galaxies, the universe is now thought to be about ten to fifteen billion years old or older. That is up from Hubbles original five or six billion a few years ago.

The determination of a star's red shift as a measure of its velocity away from the earth is done by the Doppler effect determining the increase in wavelength of the photons of a particular element such as hydrogen with a spectroscope. This wavelength will be found to have increased by an amount depending on how fast the source is traveling away from the earth. The speed of the source away from the earth is directly related to the distance from the earth by a value known as Hubbles constant Ho. This value has been increased over the years as more accurate means of its determination have been developed. Even so, Ho is now thought to be between 10 and 16 miles per second/million light years. So the distance equals the recession velocity divided by Ho. The recession velocity is determined by the number of times the hydrogen wave length has been increased. This is called a (z) factor. If the wave length is twice as long its a (z)1, three times as long (z)2, four times as long (z)3, etc. These readings must be taken above the earth's atmosphere because (z)1 photons will not penetrate the atmosphere.

If a globular cluster of gas begins to form a galaxy of stars in a relatively short time, the galaxy will be elliptical, but if the globular cluster begins to rotate and flatten into a disc because of gravity, the galaxy will form later and will be a spiral galaxy.

In any case the stars in all galaxies will condense out of separate collections of galactic gas by gravity. These collections are of various sizes and, as we shall see, their size determines the future of the stars to be formed by gravity.

First, no natural nuclear activity can be made to occur on earth. However, nuclear activity can be made to occur on earth, with a so called nuclear accelerator or with fission or fusion bombs. These nuclear activities are more complicated than we can discuss here except for the general idea of fusion. Fusion means to stick together. The fusion we should know about is the sticking together of four hydrogen atoms to make one helium atom. That is what happens in the sun to create the energy which keeps us alive. When four hydrogen atoms combine to make a helium atom, this is what happens. One hydrogen atom is one proton and one electron. Four hydrogen atoms are four protons and four electrons. One helium atom is two protons, two neutrons, and two electrons. Since one neutron is one proton and one electron, two neutrons are two protons and two electrons. Therefore, one helium atom is two protons and two electrons and two neutrons each made of one proton and one electron.

Thus, four hydrogen atoms should make one helium atom but four hydrogen atoms have a mass of 4.04 and one helium atom has a mass of only 4.00 so the difference amounts to available energy to create motion. Fortunately, this is only available in such a way as to produce excess energy at a temperature of about

10^7 Kelvin or 1.8×10^7 Rankine. These temperatures are available in stars such as the sun, so stars continue to produce excess energy which is radiated into space as long as they have plenty of hydrogen available.

At this early time the universe was much smaller and more dense than it is now and what was to become the Milky Way galaxy was one of the densely packed forming galaxies. How these galaxies expanded into the present universe is a complete mystery, for today various groups of these same galaxies are moving away from each other in what is termed uniform expansion. That means that the other galaxy groups are moving away from our galaxy group in such a manner that the farther they are from us in all directions, the faster they are moving away. So when we look at galaxies, the farthest away in all directions seem to be the galaxies formed at the beginning. Some of these distant galaxies, or perhaps they are not galaxies, are called Quasars or QSO's. A Quasar refers to a quasi stellar radio source. A QSO is a quasi stellar object. Quasi stellar means kind of star-like. Both have extremely high luminosity about 10^{12} times that of the sun. There are more than 1,000 Quasars and 20 times as many QSO's. They are more and more plentiful the farther they are from earth so they were more plentiful in the beginning. They are generally about 109 Ms with a short life of about 106 billion years. There size is less than that of the solar system. While QSOs do not emit at radio frequency they and Quasars emit through the x-ray frequency. They extend to z=4.2 but few are farther than z=3 and none are very close. However, beyond the furthest, none exist at all. Their extreme luminosity and small size leads some astronomers to believe they were black holes but this is doubtful.

Since the first stars were formed out of gas without heavy elements, they were very large and most became super novas. That means they were over ten times the mass of the sun or 10Ms and when gravity compressed the hydrogen to the ignition temperature, it rapidly formed helium which in turn burned to form element after element in the center with shells of each successively lighter element further from the center. Thus, very large super nova were the source of most all the elements heavier than helium and all elements heavier than iron. As they created elements, super nova successively contracted from the gravity of their mass and expanded from the tremendous motion of their protons, neutrons, and electrons or their extreme temperature. The activity was so great within a super nova that despite their tremendous mass, their life time was relatively short. We know that the elements in our solar system are from one or more previous super nova. The expected life of our sun is about 12 billion years. Since our solar system is about six billion years old now and the universe is from ten to fifteen billion years old or older, that leaves the difference for super novas and heavy element creation. Since the end of a super nova is a gigantic expansion an explosion which expands the gases and heavy element atoms far and wide through the galaxy and beyond, that is the source of succeeding stars which will turn out to be various sizes like our sun.

The Solar System

When our sun was formed it obviously had a disc of heavy elements and gas left over and the planets were formed of the stuff in the disc. The disc obviously had more heavy elements closer to the sun than farther away because that is the way the planets turned out to be. The inner planets called Terrestrials are Mercury, Venus, Earth, and Mars. All have partly molten iron cores surrounded by a rocky mantle and a lighter rocky crust except Mercury which has no crust. The outer planets called Jovians are Jupiter, Saturn, Uranus, Neptune and Pluto. They have rocky cores and liquid hydrogen mantles with some metal in the Jupiter and Saturn cores. They have no crust but go straight from a liquid surface to a gaseous atmosphere. No place to land.

The chart of the planet sizes compared to the earth shows the tremendous size of Jupiter and Saturn compared to the other planets. In fact, Jupiter is just barely too small to start a nuclear reaction and become a star. Also Jupiter is a liquid planet and is not collapsing by gravity. Their tremendous size is probably because of the much larger amount of gas per revolution at this much greater diameter of orbit. However, the density of gas was less for Uranus and the rest.

All the planets from the earth out have moons and the farther out you go the more rocks circling the sun with asteroids. Between Mars and Jupiter and beyond Pluto are the frozen balls that become comets when they orbit closer to the sun. With all this stuff flying around the sun, stuff has often hit the earth and the moon and probably will again unless it has all been used up.

From Mercury out, the planets are successively colder on the surface because they are farther from the sun. However they are emitting more radiation than they are absorbing from the sun and so are gradually cooling. Jupiter is only emitting about twice as much radiation as it is absorbing. In all cases the planets surface temperatures depend on their atmosphere.

The atmospheric average condition of the Terrestrial planets is shown on the chart. The total atmospheric condition on earth is complex but can readily be found in the library. An important thing about the earth's atmosphere is its ozone O_3 layer which was formed by the reaction of ultra violet radiation on the oceans before there was much oxygen in the atmosphere. The ultra violet broke the water vapor down into hydrogen and oxygen. The hydrogen left the earth and the oxygen formed an ozone O_3 layer which protected the earth from ultra violet ray penetration. An equilibrium was formed between the destruction of ozone by the ultra violet photons from the sun and the formation of ozone in the atmosphere. The conversion to an oxidizing atmosphere had to wait for life on earth.

Chart 3

Comparison of the Planets Using Earth As 1.0

Name	Dia.	Mass	Distance from sun	Chemistry	Atmosphere Temp Pressure Deg F lbs/in^2	
Mercury	.38	.055	39			
Venus	9	81	72	CO_2	850.0	1350.0
Earth	1 0	1.0	1 0	CO_2 O_2 N_2O_5	32.0	15.0
7,918 mi			93 X 10^6 mi.	H_2 H_3 H_2O		
Mars	53	.11	1.5	CO_2 N_2 Ar	10.0	.15
Jupiter	11.0	318.0	5 2	H_2 CH_4 NH_3	-282.9	
Saturn	9.4	95.0	9.5			
Uranus	4.4	15.0	19.0			
Neptune	3.9	17.0	30.0			
Pluto	.26		39.0			

Stars, Galaxies, and Clusters

Now that we know something about the formation of spiral galaxies and the formation of our solar system in a spiral galaxy we should know that most all elliptical galaxies have little gas and no dust to form new stars so they consist of mostly old stars. On that basis they must have been stars of relatively low mass since only super novas have produced mass for new stars. About seventy percent of the galaxies are spiral galaxies and the rest are elliptical galaxies and a few odd shaped galaxies. Elliptical galaxies are thought to be the oldest galaxies because they are assumed to have been formed out of large gas nebula before the nebula revolved into a rotating disc. Therefore, the stars in elliptical galaxies may be the oldest in existence.

All the stars are in galaxies and not floating around between galaxies, however almost all stars in galaxies are in clusters of stars within the galaxies. There seem to be two kinds of clusters called globular clusters and open clusters. The globular clusters which contain about 106 stars are more often in the disc of spiral galaxies. The open clusters stars generally have a higher amount of heavy elements than the globular clusters stars but the globular cluster stars are generally older than the open cluster stars. They are the oldest stars in our Milky Way galaxy. They are about twelve billion or more years old.

While most all stars may have been born in clusters, our sun is not now in a cluster and neither are many stars in our galaxy. This indicates that open cluster stars may not all remain in a cluster.

Not only do the stars in galaxies form in clusters but galaxies themselves form in cluster or groups of one kind or another with vast spaces between where no galaxies exist. However, there are many clusters of stars not exactly in but not overly far from all galaxies. Therefore, the concentrations of gas and dust within spiral galaxies extends beyond the galaxies and in between galaxies where the galaxies are in clusters. The large concentrations of gas and dust within and between galaxies in clusters has been discovered recently by the use of x-ray, ultra violet, infra red and radio viewing means above the earth's atmosphere. Without viewing with these means from above the earth's atmosphere, we will never know for sure much more about the universe.

Most people don't realize that the only stars they can see with their eyes from the surface of the earth under the best viewing conditions are stars within the Milky Way. Now think about this; until we had fairly sizeable telescopes in the year 1917 no humans had the slightest idea what the universe really was. So all of history before this time was based upon one hundred percent stupidity with respect to the background of the universe. Not until the 1920's and later did astronomers begin to realize that all of existence was composed of galaxies and that the Milky Way was just one of them. According to astronomers discoveries, the universe has become larger and older since that time. It has become much older in the last ten years based on the use of observations above the atmosphere at frequencies above and below those of light.

Visual Mental Perception

Ponder this. Humans can perceive by touch, sound, taste, smell, and sight, but only by sound and sight can they perceive from a distance and sound perception is quite limited. So let's ponder sight perception. What do we see? Sight is a mental reaction to the photons of a very limited frequency range which happen to strike our retina. All the photons which pass by our retina and don't strike it, we do not see. All those infra red and below and ultra violet and above photons we do not mentally see. We are blind to almost all photons. Even those we do see, we do not see until after they strike our retina so we really don't perceive where they came from. Ponder our blindness and think what we could see if we were not so blind. What we could see would be all the electro magnetic forces and gravity forces moving through space before us. They would be a blinding sight of forces going in every direction so that space would no longer be transparent. Blind again.

On the other hand, if our mental reaction responded to all frequencies of electro magnetic force and gravity force, we could see what we now require special equipment to see but our eyes would have to be quite large like antenna.

So, just recently astronomers are trying to see with a broader range of frequencies. As I have mentioned, a much higher density of heavy elements has been found in the space between stars and between galaxies in clusters than was previously thought to be there.

Expansion For Ever or Not

All the discussion about the expansion of the universe and the size of the galaxies and the amount of mass in the universe leads up to the main astronomical problem of the present day. The problem is that there does not appear to be nearly enough mass in all the galaxies in the universe for gravity to stop the present rate of expansion. In fact astronomers would have to find about ten times as much mass as they have so far to stop the expansion so that the universe would eventually start to contract to create a "Big Crunch." Many astronomers are searching for so called "Dark Matters" to create a "Big Crunch." The idea of a "Big Crunch" is to furnish the mass to create another "Big Bang." If astronomers could do that, they could say that a previous "Big Crunch" furnished the stuff for the last big bang. As it is, they have to get that stuff for the last big bang out of nothing and that is a bit sticky. Don't mistake me, there obviously was a source of the stuff in the universe and it is expanding so maybe you can find the answer. Not an answer but the answer. More about that later.

Hertzsprung Russell Curves

In the meantime, you should know about the nice pattern of all the stars in the universe. The pattern is in the form of curves called the Hertzsprung Russell curves. They are curves of the effective temperature of stars versus their luminosity. They should be in the dictionary but they are not even mentioned. Dictionaries are not very helpful. The curves show how stars of increasing mass also increase in temperature and luminosity and how the larger they are the shorter their life. They show how they leave the curves and become cooler and red giants and neutron stars and white dwarfs as they die depending on their mass. The red giants either become black holes, super novas, or novas and their atoms may again become stars except for black holes.

Any astronomy book in the library will have Hertzsprung Russell curves and an explanation of what they indicate except for black holes. Black holes are generally thought to be the result of gravity force on very large mass stars which have burned or emitted by explosion all of their fussionable elements so that what remains offers very little resistance to compression by gravity. Just a very large mass of heavy elements which gravity force shrinks right on through the neutron star stage into a black hole where the density of the gravity force is so great that electro magnetic photons can not escape and time stands still.

Why is The Sky Dark at Night

As long as we are pondering we might as well ponder on why the sky is dark at night. The fact that the sky is dark at night is a proof astronomers used to demonstrate that the universe is not infinite with an infinite number of stars, because if it were the sky would be as bright as the sun. If the number of stars were infinite, there would be nowhere you could look without seeing a star with another star behind it and another behind that and so on and on. So they are far away, the photons would eventually get here, each the same as when it started.

This sounds nice but that is not quite the way it is. First, we will say that all the photons which leave a star, leave radially.

Therefore, their density decreases as the square of their distance from the star. As the photon density decreases, there is more and more distance between photons. At a great distance, the lens of your eye might spend more time between photons than being hit by one; in which case you would not see the star. Further, the farther the star is away, the smaller it seems to be. For these reasons, we use big telescopes or magnifiers to make the star look larger and gather photons from an area much larger than our lens. Even so, if the stars are much further away, they will be invisible rather than just not there. Therefore, there could be any number of stars and just because the night sky is dark would have nothing to do with it. It just means we can't see good enough with the largest telescopes we have in space.

The Beginning

If the universe is limited and there are a limited number of stars and it started fifteen billion years or so ago and has expanded ever since, where did it start and where is the edge. Since astronomers can not find the place where the universe started or where the edge is, they have theories which do away with the center of the universe and the edge by curving space in time. That's not too hard to do if you do away with nothingness and replace it with whatever is between two points where it takes some time to go in some direction to get from one point to the other and both points may be in motion with respect to a lot of other points and all of them have a gravity attraction for each other and for what ever travels from the first point to the second. You got that?

Maybe not, so let's go back and further simplify the Simple Nature of Existence. Remember forces move mass through space in time and that's all there is to existence. First, we must think of mass as at least *two* things. If we only had one thing, a force could not move it through space because there would be no other thing to move it through space with respect to. Therefore, we could have no motion and if we had no motion, the only time we could have, would be before we had one thing and after we had one thing and that would certainly simplify the nature of existence. But with mass being at least two things, and we will say they are points, a force can move one point with respect to the other in a direction though space and time. Now we can expand this to lots of directions and points moved by electro magnetic and gravity forces through space in lots of times depending on which points we are talking about. So if the mass or points are things, what are the forces? They are not things, they have no mass. Forces can be instigated by things, they can travel in time through space in a direction, they can instigate the motion through space of things and [note this] forces can instigate the motion of each other in space and time. That means gravity can change the direction of an electro magnetic force. Whether an electro magnetic force can affect a gravity force or not, I believe, is unknown. So forces are instigators of the motion of stuff and forces in space and time. Now what is motion? Motion is not a thing and it is not an instigator. Motion is a *condition* of things and forces in space and time. The condition has to do with a change in the relative location in space and time of a point on a thing or a force relative to one or other points in space and time on other things or forces. So what are space and time. Space is a sort of scientific term for what is not of stuff. There is a tendency to think of space as nothingness but there may not be any nothingness in the universe. You may say nothingness is what is between photon forces because as long as their density can vary, there must be nothing between them. But what about gravity? Is there nothingness between gravity forces? Who knows?

Therefore, what is not stuff is space, which is full of forces and either is or is not partly nothingness in space.

We could talk about space and time separately because they seem to be separable. They seem to be separable because in our daily lives we omit time from observations through space. We look at an airplane and we think, there it is. But by the time we see it, it is somewhere else. This is more true of the moon and sun, and it is drastically true of distant stars. We can look through a telescope at a star that is now 13 billion years old and think, there it is. But it isn't there at all. It hasn't been there for billions of years. It created a galaxy with a sun much like our sun with a lot of planets and we will never see it because it is now many times as far away as it was when we see it now. So what is space time if we will never know about what and how things are, only about how they used to be when we see them now. Maybe we can figure out what and how things are now from the way they used to be, but then again maybe we can't. Anyway, you can see the problem space time presents in determining what is going on now and what is likely to happen in the future. Well, yes but we should consider that mass can be converted into force as in a "Hydrogen Bomb" and force can be converted into mass as "Nucleosynthesis" and force can stop time as in a "Black Hole." So, really what is the simple nature of these existence things, instigators and conditions we are talking about?

Maybe we should say "Force and Mass" moving each other through space in the "Time Force and Mass Allows." Further, we must realize that when we say moving in time, the motion of the force or mass generates the time. Time like distance is simply a means of the measurement of motion.

We hook time to photons but surely whatever motion of whatever forces or stuff are in a black hole goes on in some time even though no photons leave. Ponder that. Now to get back to earth.

Chapter 12
You Won't Believe It Anyway

Relativity is Easy

One of the ways that existence is now, that is quite different from the way we have talked about it so far, is called relativity. Relativity isn't used much because nothing we use every day moves fast enough except radiation. Radiation as you know moves at a velocity called "c". When any stuff approaches "c" velocity all the rules change. All the rules we have considered so far are called classical while the rules of relativity are called relativistic.

All the rules really are relativistic at any velocity but since the results are the same with either set of rules at normal velocities and the classical rules are easier to use, we may as well use them. We will find that the relativistic rules will lengthen time, shorten distance and increase mass as we approach "c" velocity. In fact, these changes are so drastic that time would stand still, distance would dissipate and mass would go to infinity if we did go to "c" velocity. Therefore, we don't.

To get a better idea of the affect velocity has on space and time ponder this:

Space Clock

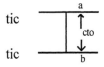

A man "M" stays still on earth and a woman "W" travels away in a space ship at a velocity "v". The woman "W" has a clock with a hand that travels from "a" to "b" for each tic of the space clock at the speed of light "c". A fast clock. The woman "W" sees the hand go from "a" to "b" for each tic in time "to", so her distance from "a" to "b" is "cto", But "M" looks at the clock through a telescope and sees the hand go from "a", to "b", for each tic because after the hand leaves "a" the clock moves though space at a velocity "v" for a distance of S = Vt. From a Pythagorean rule about triangles which says in Fig. 1:

$$H^2 = A^2 + B^2 \text{ or } H = \sqrt{A^2 + B^2}$$

The long side H of a right angle ($90°$) triangle equals the square root of the sum of the squares of the other two sides. Then, since Cto, S and Ct are sides of a right triangle where S=Vt we can say:

$(ct)^2 = (cto)^2 + (vt)^2$ divided both sides of the equation by c^2

$t^2 = t^2 o^2 + (Vt/c)^2$ transfer $(Vt/c)^2$ to the other side.

$t^2 o^2 = t^2 - (Vt/c)^2$ divide both sides by t^2

$t^2 o^2 / t^2 = 1 - (v/c)^2$ take square root of both sides

$to/t = \sqrt{1 - (v/c)^2}$

This is based on a standard conversion function for changing from classical to relativistic rules. It is called the gamma γ function.

where $\gamma = 1/\sqrt{1 - v^2/c^2}$

Gamma is a Greek letter. Wherever velocity "v" is a normal velocity gamma equals one, but when "v" approaches "c" gamma approaches infinity.

To see what this means, assume the woman's velocity is one half the velocity of light "c" then

$to/t = \sqrt{1-(1/2)^2} = \sqrt{1 - .25} = \sqrt{.75}$

$to/t = .866$ or $to = .866t$

Which says that the woman's time is only .866 as fast as the man's time. So, as you have probably heard, as long as the woman keeps going at one half the speed of light she will age only .866 as fast as the man. However, the woman will not feel that her time is a bit different than it has every been. What will be different is what she sees when she looks through her telescope back at the man. He will seem to be moving slower just like she is.

By the same relativistic rules the sum of two velocities in the same direction can not exceed "c" the velocity of light and of all radiation. For instance, if the woman's son took off from the woman's space ship in the same direction at "S," one half the speed of light "c" faster than the woman "W" then you might think that be would be traveling at the speed of light away from the earth. However, this is not the case. The son's speed "S" from the earth would be:

$$S = \frac{S^1 + V}{1 + \frac{S_1 V}{c^2}} \qquad \text{or} \qquad \frac{.5c + .5c}{1 + \frac{.5c \times .5c}{c^2}}$$

$$S = \frac{c\,(.5 + .5)}{1 + \frac{.25c^2}{c^2}} \qquad \text{or} \qquad \frac{c}{1.25} \quad = .8c$$

the derivation of this determination of the son's speed "s" is beyond the scope of this book. It is from Feynman's *Lecture on Physics*.

The son's time with respect to the man's time would be:

$$to/t = \sqrt{1 - \left(\frac{.8c}{c}\right)^2} \quad = \sqrt{1 - .8^2} \quad = \sqrt{.36}$$

which says that the son's time is only .6 as fast as the man's time. So, the son will age only .6 times as fast as the man.

Now you may think that this process should be reversible and that we should be able to think of the woman or her son as stationary with the man and the earth speeding away. In this case it would be the man on earth who aged more slowly. That's relativity isn't it? Well not exactly. The man is on a planet which is a part of a solar system which is a part of a galaxy which is part of a universe which has a rather fixed relationship in space with respect to gravity. Even though the galaxies are expanding, they are expanding uniformly. Further, as the galaxies expand away from the earth, the time on each one is slower with respect to earth, based on its speed away from earth. This speed causes the decrease in the frequency of its photons as they strike the earth and are so called, "red shifted."

So your time with respect to your surroundings will depend on whether you are in a relatively fixed position with respect to the uniform expansion of the universe, or whether you are moving rapidly with respect to the uniform expansion of the universe. Astronomers say, "with respect to the fixed stars."

To check what would happen if we did not change the classic rules to relativistic rules when the velocity was "c" or higher, the highest voltage possible was used to force an electron to go as fast as it would go under the classic rule of:

$E = \frac{1}{2} MV^2$

The force applied on the electron under the classic rule:

$F = MA$

should have accelerated the electron to a velocity of 198% of "c". However, the electron actually only went 98% of the velocity of "c". The rest of the energy "E" increased the mass "Mo" of the electron in accordance with

$$M = \frac{Mo}{\sqrt{1 - \frac{v^2}{c^2}}} = \frac{Mo}{\sqrt{1 - .96}} = \frac{Mo}{.2} = 5\,Mo$$

where "Mo" was the original mass and "M" was the final mass which increased to five times the original mass rather than go faster than the velocity of "c".

In the future when we learn to control the nuclear fusion of hydrogen to make helium so that a tremendous amount of energy is available from a very small mass, we really can go cruising away from the earth in a space ship at, let's say, one half the velocity of "c". But in the real world, the first thing we must do is to accelerate up to the velocity of .5 "c". This will take quite a while so our rate of acceleration must be such that we are comfortable during this time. Let's say we accelerate at one "G" so we will feel just like we are on earth. One "G" is one times the force of gravity and is therefore an acceleration of 32.3 ft/sec². This gravity force will be in the direction opposite the direction in which we are traveling. The time required to get up to .5 "G" will be $T = V/_A$ or $T = 93,000 \times 5280/32.2 = 15.25 \times 10^6$ sec. or 4,236 hours or 177 days or 6 months. Of course when we come home from our journey we will have to decelerate at one "G" for six months before we can land on earth.

Now, once we get up to a speed of .5 "c" or 93,000 miles per sec., we will have gone $D = 1/2 VT = 1/2\ 93,000 \times 15.25 \times 10^6$ or 709×10^9 or 709 billion miles classical. At this velocity, it would be further relativistically. We left the solar system at about 4 billion miles so it is long gone and we might as well visit our closet star neighbors to see if there are any livable planets there. Our closest star neighbors are four light years and seven light years away.

Can we make it there and back?

Well, we can use our gamma equation to shorten the distance so:

$$D = Do\sqrt{1 - \frac{v^2}{c^2}}$$

or

$$D = 240,000\sqrt{1 - \frac{v^2}{c^2}} = 240,000\sqrt{1 - .25} = 240,000\sqrt{.75}$$

$$D = 240,000 \times .866 = 207,846 \text{ miles}$$

Since our one year acceleration and deceleration time will take us 24 light years distance, we can say our two distance choices are: Do_1 = 4 light years x 2 - .24 = 7.76 light years

Do_2 = 7 light years x 2 - .24 = 13.76 light years

Then at .5 "c" the distance will be:

D_1 = 7.76 x .866 x 2 = 13.44 light years

D_2 = 13.76 x .866 x 2 = 23.83 light years

Then at .5 "c" our time will be:

T_1 = 13.44 + 1 = 14.44 years

T_2 = 23.83 + 1 = 24.83 years

Note that these are traveler times. Earth times will be about 1/.866 or about 15% longer.

So yes we can make it but first we must figure out how to utilize fusion energy. So get busy.

Gravity Effect on Time

Besides motion, time is changed by a variation in the distance to the center of a large mass so that the force of gravity is changed. On the surface of a neutron star where gravity is one billion times that of earth's surface, time is calculated to be about 20 percent slower while at the surface of a black hole, time would stand still. Thus gravity affects photons in the same way motion affects photons. At the surface of a black hole, no photon force is strong enough to leave and that is why black holes are called black. Since black holes are invisible, the only way they can become discovered is by the reaction of their surroundings. When one of a pair of binary stars is a black hole and the other star is orbiting it and its mass is feeding into it, you can assume you are looking at a black hole if it were not invisible.

Time and Measurement

When we consider the variations of time because of velocity with respect to "c" or because of gravity with respect to mass, we are using various means to determine time. Actually, we can determine time anyway we wish since time's only meaning to us must be somehow connected to our very short life times. Our only means of comparing times is by some kind of measurement. The only kind of measurement we have thought of has to do with counting repetitive cycles such as days or years or light years. However, if these repetitive cycles themselves change, in time, then our concept of total time is wrong. Note, that time itself hasn't changed, it's our concept of time that has gone astray because our repetitive cycles have changed time.

On this basis, we might think of a better way of measuring time than by using repetitive cycles which themselves change time in time when their surrounding conditions change. After all, if a change in surrounding conditions can change the repetitive cycle times themselves, we don't know for sure whether time itself changed or whether just the repetitive cycle time changed. Ponder this, because you may find that when you travel through space at close to photon speed, time doesn't care whether you measure it or not. Then too, I doubt that "Black Holes" will last any longer because photons do not leave their surface. However, I will never know for sure.

Now there is a word called simultaneous which means at the same time and many things in life seem to be simultaneous but really are not quite, because of the speed of light and our nervous system. Our perception of existence is constantly time delayed but we tend to ignore it. We pretend that we live in the here and now and it is difficult to take the time delay into consideration, especially the cosmic time delay. For instance, we know that what we see of quasars is where they were more than six to ten billion years ago. So, where are they today?

No one on Earth will ever see where any quasars are today because the Earth and the Sun will be gone before any photons leaving a quasar today will ever get here. Today the quasars are almost twice as far away as they were when we see them. That makes the universe quite a bit larger since they are on the outer fringe and have been traveling radially at about the speed of light for the ten or fifteen billion years since we see them today.

However, there must be a simultaneous time even if we cannot perceive it. We can imagine a simultaneous universal time with difficulty. Such a simultaneous universal imaginary time does not change pace from place to place or from condition to condition. Whether the real time does or not, I really don't know.

Chapter 13
This Is What Scientists Say

Backward in Time and The Cosmological Principle

So, how does all this make space time curved. Well, from here on earth we can look in any direction and see what is believed to be galaxies formed some time after hydrogen and helium clumping, then no matter in which direction we look, if we look far enough we are looking at the first galaxies formed. If this is true here in the Milky Way it must be true in all galaxies because they were all formed at about the same time. If this is true in all the galaxies, then no matter where anyone in the universe looks, all other clusters of galaxies are separating at a rate proportional to their distance apart and the furthest ones in all directions are essentially in the same relative position as when they were formed at that time. If someone on a planet of the star from the super nova of the 13 billion year old star we looked at, were to look at us now; they would see the quasar which produced a galaxy which produced a super nova from which our sun was formed, and they would see it back at the time of its beginning where it was then. This says that at any instant, at any place in the universe, you could look in any direction and the universe would look just the same. This is called the "Cosmological Principle." So no matter which way we look, it is backwards in time. If there were some direction in which we could look and see the future, we would have it made. Since we can't look anywhere but backward, we have no choice if we wish to look through space time at all. So space is curved to the rear until we can see the future. But this is not the space curvature we are talking about.

If you expect to see the "Big Bang" past in one specific

direction in space, what do you expect to see when you look into space in the opposite direction? If your answer is nothing, then you are in the wrong place in the universe. At least that's what most astronomers thought until recently when the Cosmological Principle has come into question.

"Big Bang" Nucleosynthesis and Uniform Expansion

Let's ponder the Cosmological Principle based on our simple nature of existence taken step by step. Let's take space first. Assume existence consists of nothing but space. No mass, no forces and therefore no motion. So what use is time. Now how are we going to curve space when it is nothing and there is no time? Now let's take mass second. Assume existence exists of nothing but mass. Solid mass with no atoms, no space, no forces or motion and only two times. Before and after the mass. Now let's take forces third. If there is no mass, can there be forces? Apparently if the forces are photons or radiation there can be photons only and time. At least the "Big Bang" theory says so. It says there was a tremendous amount of radiation which is supposed to be photons going somewhere at a velocity of "c" with a tremendous density which is equivalent to an extremely high temperature. Any extreme temperature at the beginning must have been from extreme density because radiation frequency is limited by a critical frequency beyond which the energy falls to zero. See Fig. 4. The motion of the photons supposedly started at a point the "Big Bang" theory says. So that point is where time started and where the photons started which by nucleosynthesis created what has turned out to be the mass of the universe. Nucleosynthesis is a scientific term for the change of radiation energy into mass. Whether there was gravity before there was mass is questionable. At any rate, the only direction in which the radiation could expand from a point would be radially and the only thing radial expansion from a point can create is a sphere. Now expansion is one thing but uniform expansion is quite another. Uniform expansion means radial as well as peripheral expansion. We assume that means the expansion of all the volume within the sphere and not the expansion of a spherical shell. So uniform radial as well as peripheral expansion of radiation requires a continuous supply of photons expanding from the point and it requires that the photons constantly accelerate radially to keep the same separation radially that they have peripherally. This is contrary to the concept that photons move at one constant velocity. Therefore, nucleosynthesis must take place almost immediately if uniform radial expansion is to take place.

Where is the Radial Expansion Force?

In this case if radial expansion of electrons and protons took place at a rate to match peripheral expansion there must have been a constant radial force to create the radial acceleration necessary for uniform expansion. But where did this force come from. Certainly not from the "Big Bang" which took place before nucleosynthesis occurred.

So that we don't become confused by the concept of radial, spherical, uniform expansion of *radiation* from a point, let's just say that it is impossible and say that the radial, spherical expansion of radiation or photons was at the velocity "C" of photons and was not uniform expansion. As this expansion took place the photon density decreased by nucleosynthesis and by expansion to the background radiation of about 5 degrees Rankine today. Until recently, this background radiation has seemed to be the same in all directions. However, recently there have been readings from above the earth's atmosphere which indicate a directionality or gradient to this background radiation as there should be. Science says that for the first minute the photon density, and therefore the temperature, was so great that electrons and positrons were formed and their interaction again formed photons so that the photon expansion was somewhat slowed down. A positron is like an electron but it is attracted to an electron so that when they come together, energy is released to form two photons. These again formed electrons and protons. Science says those reactions furnished the energy for the uniform spherical expansion of the electrons and protons and prevented the photons from expanding radially at "C" the speed of radiation.

Eventually, however, when the temperature was cool enough

for the electrons to join with the protons to make hydrogen and to make neutrons so helium could form, the free electrons ran out and the universe became clear enough for photons to travel in a straight line. At this temperature no more positrons are formed to react with electrons so where the energy came from to accelerate protons and electrons radially to match their peripheral expansion is a mystery.

There It Is. To solve this mystery, scientists have determined that the Doppler affect is caused by motions through space but the red shifts of galaxies are caused by the expansion of space itself not the expansion of galaxies through space. Therefore, galaxies are not getting farther apart, rather the space between galaxies is stretching. Evidently, no force is required to stretch space. Further, space isn't only stretching, it is curving so what seems to be the affect of gravity and centrifugal force is really simply curved space. This curvature of space also prevents the universe from having an outer edge. This is the curvature we have been talking about.

This solution to the mystery of the missing acceleration force for uniform expansion sounds nice but I personally have trouble with the curved space between my foot and the scale when I weigh myself. But, assuming this is true, and the universe continued to cool as space expanded and curved. Then hydrogen and helium began to clump so that probably Quasars and QSO's could form. So this is as far back as we can see today and it was about 13 or so billion years ago and the quasars were leaving us at about 95% of "c" the speed of light as we see their photons today. At that time the stuff of our Milky Way galaxy was probably another Quasar and much closer to the Quasars whose photons we see today. So all we can see today is about a 13 billion or so light year radius sphere into the past that 13 billion years ago was apparently much smaller because space has been expanding uniformly ever since. This is all of the universe we can see, so we really can't be sure what is beyond this sphere. To us it looks black. But almost all of the stars look black if we don't have a large enough telescope. Could we see any further back in time if we had a 200 inch telescope in space?

The answer is yes, if there is anything to see and there should be in some direction.

Chapter 14
This Is What I Say

Big Bang Constant Velocity, Constant Density, Uniform Expansion Concept

This concept solves the Uniform Expansion mystery without an acceleration force and without stretching space. It is based only on forces Moving Stuff Through Space in time or the Simple Nature of Existence.

First, we will start with the "Big Bang" force directly after nucleosynthesis which is causing the universe of stuff to move radially away from the location of the "Big Bang." Since the initial "Big "Bang force is the greatest, the first amount of stuff to move per unit if time will be the greatest and will move radially at the greatest velocity. The next amount of stuff to move will be a little less dense and will move radially at a slightly lower velocity because the "Big Bang" force is slightly lower. And so as that "Big Bang" force decreases the stuff will move radially at lower and lower density and lower and lower velocity and the radial "Big Bang" force will decrease until that of today.

The decrease in leaving density will match the decrease in peripheral density from expansion and the decrease in leaving velocity will cause the radially increasing separation of stuff to just match the peripheral increasing separation of stuff. This can be shown on the two following charts which should make the concept easy to understand. See chart 4.

Chart 4

How Constant Velocities Can Produce Uniform Expansion

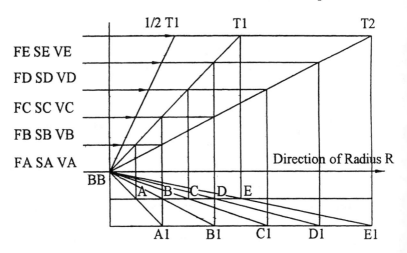

All stuff leaves from BB the "Big Bang" location and travels in the direction of a radius R. The greatest force F_E gives the densest stuff S_E the greatest velocity V_E.

The next greatest force F_D gives the next densest stuff S_D the next greatest velocity V_D.

The next greatest force F_C — etc. etc. to the force F_A gives the least dense stuff S_A the least velocity VA before we get to the present condition at BB the Big Bang location.

After time T_1, A, B, C, D, and E are as far apart as shown traveling along the direction of a radius from BB.

After time T_2 which is twice T_1, A, B, C, D, and E are as far apart as shown by A_1, B_1, C_1, D_1, and E_1, which is twice as far apart as at T_1.

This is uniform expansion at constant velocity.

Explanation of Chart 5

In the "Universe Section Chart" of a Universal Sphere all lettered points are traveling radially away from the center "O" at constant velocities proportional to their radii. Also, all lettered points are traveling peripherally away from each other at velocities in proportion to their radii. Thus, contrary to the way it looks, all lettered points are traveling away from each other at velocities in proportion to their distance apart.

Calculations using distance for velocity, will show that the velocity at radius "OI" divided by the velocity at radius "OJ" is equal to the velocity at radius "OJ" divided by the velocity at radius "OK". Therefore, if point "J" were considered stationary, point "I" would be traveling away from point "J" toward point "Y" and point "K" would be traveling away from point "J" toward point "O" in proportion to their radial distances apart. Further, when "N" gets to "M" and "J" gets to "I", "N" and "J" will be "W" farther apart peripherally. When "N" gets to "M" and "P" gets to "N", "N" and "P" will be "W" further apart radially.. Therefore, all lettered points increase in velocity from each other as they increase in distance from each other both peripherally and radially.

These charts do not consider the force of gravity which should make radial expansion a little slower than peripheral expansion. This could have been the condition which instigated the clumping of hydrogen so that the local affect of gravity could create galaxies.

Uniformly Decreasing Uniform Universal Density

An increase in areas 1, 2, 3, and 4 causes a peripheral decrease in the density of stuff at each of these radii which is proportional to the square of each radius. Also, at each of these radii the radial density is decreasing as each successively lower velocity and density goes by. Therefore, the density of stuff decreases as the square of the radius peripherally and directly as the radius radially or as the cube of the radius totally. Thus, the overall density of the spherical universe decreases as the cube of its radius or directly as its volume.

This "Section Chart" shows how the maintenance of a uniform decreasing universal density and a uniform expansion of all the stuff in the inverse can take place simultaneously under this concept and only under this concept. Contrary to what Einstein says; you will see that this concept does not violate the "Cosmological Principal." In fact, this concept creates the "Cosmological Principle."

Universe Section Chart 5

"Big Bang" Spherical, Radial & Peripheral Expansion

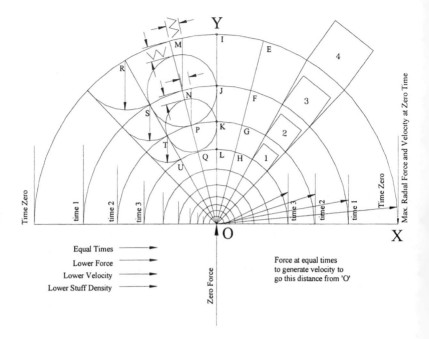

The Latest Cosmological Finding

On the evening of February 27, 1998 on the News Hour with Jim Lehrer television program, a cosmologist reported on a startling new cosmological discovery about the expansion of the Universe. He stated that their recent measurements indicated that the recent rate of universal expansion was more rapid than the early rate of universal expansion. He then brought up the cosmological problem this finding created because they thought the force of gravity would slow down the universal rate of expansion and now they have no idea where a force would come form to increase the recent rate of universal expansion.

Now you know what the new cosmological problem is and we will show how the new concept of "Constant Velocity Uniform Expansion" of the universe solves the problem. Remember I pointed out that gravity would somewhat decease the radial velocity and thereby cause clumping. Well, consider that the earliest clumps to leave radially had the greatest mass, the greatest velocity and were slowed by the greatest gravity since these clumps were close to the greatest density that the universe would ever have. As time went on, the later forming clumps would be less dense, their radial velocity would be less and their gravity braking force would be less and less since they would be surrounded by a greater and greater gravity balancing mass.

On this basis the oldest or earliest expansion mass on the outer periphery of the universe will always have the greatest braking force. Therefore, the new cosmological problem is not that the recent rate of universal expansion is speeding up, it is that the old rate of cosmological expansion on the outer periphery of the universe is still slowing down faster than inner rate.

This finding indicates that we are located somewhat centrally in the universe. It further illustrates that there is no expansion force required as illustrated in my concept of a "Constant Velocity Uniform Expansion" of the universe.

The Center and the Edge

We have covered the general "Big Bang" concept where in the universe started from a point and uniformly expanded without having a center or an outer edge. The reason for the lack of a center or an edge is because they were never found. This has been explained by the concept that space is curved. Since everything in the universe follows the curvature of space we can't find an end to the curve or what would be an edge.

Now as I have explained, I don't believe this is true and I believe we can find the center and the edge of the universe. The latest cosmological finding we just discussed is one proof that I am correct. Actually we have had the proof all along and did not recognize it. The proof lies in the Quasars. They were obviously the first tremendously dense , tremendously bright objects away from the center of the "Big Bang." Now there are no quasars close to us and beyond quasars we see nothing. I believe we can see nothing but quasars in the ten to fifteen billion light years distance. Therefore, Quasars define the edge of our viewing distance and should be where the outer edge of the universe was ten to fifteen billion years ago. Since the Quasars were at the outer edge of the universe, their expansion velocity away from the center was slowed by the gravity force of the whole universe much more than the galaxies in the central part of the universe where their expansion velocities were much less affected by gravity.

If we wish to find the center of the universe, we have but to plot the distance of all the furthest quasars from the Milky Way in all directions possible. This should establish a semi spherical surface, the center of which should be the center of the universe. Maybe this information is already available. If it is, I would certainly like to know about it.

As soon as we determine that the Universe is a sphere and its density increases from its center to its periphery because of gravity even though it's expansion is essentially uniform we can realize that the greatest density of the universe is represented by the quasars which are only visible because of their tremendous density and luminosity. All other galaxies would be invisible at quasar distance. The present distance to what we now see as quasars and all galaxies is almost twice what it was at the time we see them. But the quasars, what ever they are now, have expanded the slowest. Even so, we should remember that the age of the universe includes the time everything took to get where we see it now plus the time the photons take to get from there to her. Since the photons all go the same velocity, the only difference is in the velocity toward the center of the universe and the velocity away from the center of the universe. Therefore, the rate of expansion in the center of the universe which is closer and therefore younger, seems to be faster than the rate of expansion toward the outer periphery which is further and therefore older.

I pointed this out in my reference to the News Hour broadcast with Jim Lehrer. Now I refer to *Science News* vol. 153 *The Weekly News Magazine of Science under Astronomy* on page 344. Living with lamda the cosmological constant. It's the antigravity force invented by Einstein when he developed his General Relativity concept. Later he removed it. Now the Institute for Advance Study in Princeton, NJ, first finished a study which shows exactly what I have just told you, but since they can't understand it, they dredge up lamda the anti gravity force to explain it. The article has to do with their hatred of lamda.

Chart 6

We Are Late Comers

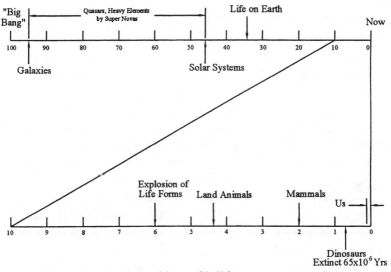

Percent of the age of the Universe
This chart is in accordance with present science

Chapter 15
Lately We Are Part of the Universe

To summarize our place on earth with respect to the universe and to life on this earth, you can see from chart #6 that we are relatively late comers. The total width of chart 6 is now thought to be from thirteen to fifteen billion years. You can readily see what an insignificant part of the time the universe has been in existence that humans have been in existence. You can readily see from this chart that the universe can exist very well with or without life on one of its insignificant planets; especially human life which has barely come into existence at all.

Now where do you think humans got the idea that this universe was made for them? This is like the flea thinking the elephant was made for him. Humans surely must realize that the universe will go right on after our sun novas and the earth is gone. Even if humans can learn to travel through space and find a suitable planet around a younger sun, the probable continued universal expansion will do away with the present concept of life.

However, I am somewhat skeptical that humans will have any of these problems. The present social problems of earthly humans seem to be developing into the demise of human existence and I wonder if the masses of humans who are developing on this planet will ever have the intelligence to do what is required to continue human existence.

The basic reason I have written this book is to encourage the young people of this planet to become intelligent enough to follow a social concept that will change the direction of human behavior. Therefore, the rest of this book will have to do with the simple nature of the social existence of each human with respect to all other humans based on what scientists have found out recently.

Chapter 16
We Can't Make Truth

The Simple Nature of Social Existence

The simple nature of the social existence of humans on this earth at the present time depends on the beliefs of humans societies which have absolutely no knowledge of what this book has covered so far except for the few true scientists. Therefore, if you wish to be knowledgeable concerning the nature of social existence on this earth, you will have to abandon the false present social concepts and seek the truth. You may not like the truth. You may prefer to accept the present false social concepts. If this is so, do not read any farther. However, if you wish to know the truth, read on. You can always stop.

What Do We Mean by Truth

First we must develop a solid understanding of what we mean by truth. That means we must agree on the meaning of the words we use. No tricks, no double meanings. When we say up, we mean away from the center of the earth and when we say down, we mean toward the center of the earth. When we say "truth", we mean that which can be proven to exist through the evaluation thought and test process carried to the extreme in all directions until the result reaches a practical identity with that which actually exists. That which actually exists is forces moving mass through space in time according to proven natural laws and no other way. Thus, radiation has a velocity regardless of what scientists say it is. If they say the velocity of radiation in a vacuum is 186,272 miles a second and that is the actual velocity of radiation, then what scientists say, is the truth. However, if scientists made a slight error, the speed of radiation does not change and what scientists say, is not true. The truth which exists is the actual speed of radiation regardless of what scientists say or believe it to be. No amount of faith in their tests will change it.

The statement that "the truth exists" must therefore be accepted, since that which exists is simply the definition of truth. That which does not exist is considered to be non-existent and not truth.

Therefore we can say,

Truth exists. Truth must be found and proven. Truth can not be created or pre-determined.

Truth exists regardless of what humans say or write or believe. Thus, the saying or writing or believing has absolutely no affect on truth.

To find truth, humans must perceive, experience, test and verify. If the finding turns out to be true, it was true before it was found. The truth does not become truth with the finding.

The acquisition of documentary evidence which establishes an identity between our idea of the truth of a concept and its actual truth can never assure their identity since all evidence can be incomplete or inaccurate. However, to the extent that incompleteness and inaccuracy can be overcome, an identity will be more likely.

All thought in the learning process consists of a series of evaluation as:

Believe-question-test-accept

or believe-question-test-reject

or believe-question-test-hold

These evaluations must be made of each part of an idea or concept and may have various results as:

An acceptance of the concept as a whole

or a rejection of the concept as a whole

or a change in the concept by rejection of part and acceptance of part

or withholding for further evaluation

The results of these evaluation thought processes have absolutely no affect on the actual truth or falseness of the concept, but they do determine our idea of its truth or falseness. If the evaluation thought process is carried to extreme by a series of question and test steps in all directions, eventually adequate documentary evidence may be acquired to establish an identity between our idea of the truth of a concept and its actual truth. The most likely example of the identity of our idea of the truth and the actual truth lies in mathematics.

Faith, as an unquestioning belief, may be equated to the acceptance of an assumption which is considered true until proven false. In this sense, to be useful in the thought process, faith must have a time limit after which it is questioned. If no time limit is applied and no questioning takes place through a succession of evaluation thought processes, there can be no documentary evidence acquired to establish an identity with truth or the lack of such an identity.

The acquisition of documentary evidence which established an identity between our idea of the truth of a concept and its actual truth can never assure their identity since all evidence can be incomplete, inaccurate or false. However, to the extent that incompleteness and inaccuracy can be overcome: to this extent an identity can be more likely.

Only through the eventual rejection of any concept as truth without documentary evidence to establish its identity with truth, can the thought process of learning take place. Only through the thought process of learning can adequate documentary evidence eventually be acquired to establish an identity between concepts and truth.

Knowledge

The amount of knowledge which would be found to be truth as determined by the evaluation thought process carried to extreme by a series of question and test steps in all directions until adequate documentary evidence is acquired to establish an identity with actual truth, would probably be small compared to what man considers to be his store house of knowledge. Much of what man believes to be knowledge, would be found to be untrue and much would be found to be inconclusive as to its truth. The inconclusiveness of much of mans knowledge is apparent by the tremendous amount of contradictory so called knowledge. This is not inconsistent since there is nothing about most non technical knowledge which attests to its truth. Much knowledge simply exists to be accepted or rejected at will. Once accepted, man rationalizes this knowledge as truth even though it may conflict with other similar knowledge he has accepted. In many areas, man tends to accept opinions, concepts and fiction as knowledge because to refuse to do so would require some form of evaluation thought process. The evaluation thought process in non technical fields of knowledge is often restricted by taboo and in other fields by fear of the unknown and laziness.

Notice that in social discussion, the terms "man", "men", "he", and "mankind" are used to refer to humans of both sexes combined. I have used these standard terminologies to try to keep from being too different.

The first and most important step to determine knowledge of truth is to admit a lack of knowledge where truth has not been determined. "I do not know" seem most difficult for leaders of man to say. Most leaders of man seem psychologically compelled to appear to know everything with little regard for truth. The finding of truth by a suitably intensive evaluation thought process is most difficult and more often than not - not achievable in a short span of time. It is, therefore, not a suitable psychological endeavor for the leaders of men. Down through the ages, the leaders of men have required answers for the questions of their followers. These questions in many areas have remained essentially the same while the answers have gone through successive stages of variation and are still. Rare is the leader who has ever said "I do not know."

Until mankind realizes that most of his knowledge in non technical fields is without truth, he will not seek truth in these fields. Therefore, you will generally not learn the truth in non technical fields. The total of mankind's' non technical knowledge which does have an identity with truth is probably astoundingly small.

My intention is not to tear down without rebuilding or to take away without replacing, but in many fields of knowledge, I have no choice. I suggest you tear down and take away knowledge which is found to be untrue by the evaluation and thought process of question and test. The knowledge which is found to withstand all evaluation and to have an identity with truth will remain.

The deletion of all untrue knowledge and the labeling of all inconclusive knowledge will undoubtedly leave large unknown and questionable areas of no knowledge. We cannot replace all the knowledge, which is proved to be untrue, with new truths. The truth cannot be created, it must be found. The truth exists, but until it is found, any substitute is worse than nothing. A substitute for the truth tends to be accepted for the actual truth and thereby thwarts an adequate search for the truth.

The leaders of men who offer substitute truths, do so to bolster their leadership. They often offer substitute truths on the basis that they are self evident or divinely inspired and therefore should be accepted as truth on faith without the evaluation thought process of question and test. Substitute truth presented on this basis is very easy to accept compared to the effort required to continue the search and compared to the quandary of remaining in the unknown. Those who offer substitute truths have created a tremendous trap into which mankind has fallen and where he remains.

My main purpose is to inspire mankind to want to get out of the trap. From there he must find his own way toward the truth.

The Nature of False Truth

Since the beginning of history man has created false truth as well as found truth. Some of the false truth has been disproved but most remains. Some of the false truths of history were at one time believed by about every living man who could think.

The earth is flat.

The earth is the central planet with the sun and all the stars revolving around it.

If believing could create truth because of the majority who believe or the strength of conviction, this would have done it.

Most of the stories of all beliefs concerning the miraculous origin of man and prophet.

Most of the stories of all beliefs concerning the origin and existence of devils, demons and witches.

The medical concept of blood oscillation in the body.

The space concept of an ether filled void is within my life time.

Most of the concepts of most philosophers delve into the supernatural and therefore fall into the category of "False Truth."

Most of mankind continues to believe in the coexistence of natural and supernatural, and therefore, perpetuates "False Truth."

Humans continue to believe that if they proclaim strongly enough and believe devoutly enough that somehow a change in natural laws will occur and create truth, contrary to true natural laws.

Once man has found and accumulated a sufficient number of truths in any field, he can combine these truths in to various relationships. The relationships of combined truths make possible the creation of things which did not previously exist such as a wheel or a television. Some of these things make possible the finding of new truths. Things like microscopes, telescopes, x-ray, microchip, equipment for probing the earth and space, and equipment for probing extremely high and low temperature and pressure effects on substances; these things tell man the truth about the natural laws which control him and his surroundings. These are examples of the kinds of things which are used in the process of truth searching for physical truths. This process has been found to be accumulative in the recent past so that man has found more physical truth in the last few years than in all previous recorded history. This is probably just the beginning if. There is a very large if. If man can create a new and improved individual and international system which puts more premium on finding and utilizing truth to determine good and bad than on utilizing false truth.

Good and Bad, Right and Wrong

Mankind has not yet established for itself a consistent concept of good and bad behavior. Rather there are many inconsistent concepts through out the world. The goodness or badness of a particular behavior depends on which set of concepts are used to judge the behavior.

Examples of conflicting concepts:

1. Concepts established by various beliefs with regard to food, medicine, dress, work, birth control, etc.
2. Concepts established by various governments with respect to patriotism, free speech, capitol punishment, individual rights, taxes, etc.
3. Concepts determined by self preservation in social relationships, in business relationships, in success and adversity in society.
4. Concepts determined by the natural desires of the human body with respect to social acceptance in various societies.
5. Concepts determined by each man for himself out of the hodge podge of the preceding concepts.

Because of the conflicting concepts of good and bad behavior, mankind probably cannot exist in a society without some rules of behavior called law. These rules or laws have been built up in time until they consist of a running record of what has previously been decided as right and wrong behavior. The right or wrongness according to these laws was probably connected with some concept of good and bad behavior when the laws were originally formulated. However, in time laws maintain their right and wrong authority whether they maintain their connection with good and bad or not. Occasionally this becomes obvious and the laws are changed.

Thus, the terms right and wrong generally refer to legal behavior and good and bad to moral behavior. While the intent of mankind may be for the legal and moral to go hand-in-hand with the right and good against the wrong and bad, such has not always been the case.

The one great legal correction, which is about the only indication that mankind has the power mentally to correct itself, consists of the abolition of slavery and bondage or the legal right of one individual to own another physically.

To parallel the legal rules of right and wrong, there are moral rules of good and bad. Unlike the legal rules which are a running record and subject to change as society changes, the moral rules are more fixed and not readily subject to change as society changes. The fixed position of moral rules is derived from the supposed dependence of moral behavior on religion and the dependence of religion on dogma. Since the moral rules are not readily updated for the requirements of social changes, the legal rules are made without adequate moral support. Thus, the German people accepted Hitler's laws and the United States southern people accept the racism of Governor Wallace. These are examples of the ease with which right and wrong as exemplified by laws may become disassociated with good and bad.

The dictionary definition of "dogma" is, "a point of view or tenet put forth as authoritative without adequate grounds."

Chapter 17 Control or Follows

The Means of Animal Control

Many animal species live in some form of group. The existence of animal groups indicates that these animals derive more advantage from group existence than from separate existence. The advantage derived would logically be a greater assurance of the continuation of the species from both the survival of the individual through protection, hunting requirements and the survival of the group through reproduction.

These groups take various forms such as:

1. Family groups
   Separate family for a specific area
   Migratory or non-migratory
   Multi-family in an area
   Migratory or non-migratory
2. Herd or School Groups
   Migratory or non-migratory

For the groups to function, requires some form of relationships between the individuals of the groups. The status of these relationships are manifold but they are almost all based on individual combat or the threat of individual combat. In the case of the separate family for a specific area, the prize of combat is the best area or domain. In the other cases the prize is the leadership of the group. The combat for domain or leadership almost never results in death except by accident. Once domain or leadership has been established, it is maintained by threat of combat until a new owner or leader is established by combat. The threat of combat is a form of fear. Any individual of the group may challenge the leader. Only fear of failure prevents such a challenge.

The controller or leader thus established by combat becomes the controller of the other individuals of the group. The other individuals in the group will be called the controlled. In many cases the group welfare may depend on the capability of the controller since he becomes more or less responsible for the controlled. Whether the group welfare is best served by determining its leadership by combat may be questionable. However, this seems to be the general means of determination.

Not only is the group leadership determined by combat, but generally a system of controller-controlled is established by combat or threat of combat throughout the group. While this controller-controlled system would probably not be a chain of command, it would be considered by the group as the order of relative privilege or priority or perhaps of importance to the survival of the group. As humans evolved, they must have evolved some means of group control wherein the order was determined by individual combat. As humans evolved and became more complex, so did their control systems.

The Means of Human Control

As humans evolved they eventually developed a means of establishing control which were the first based on mental capability rather than on physical capability and, therefore, more sophisticated than by individual combat. While victory in individual combat requires some mental capability as well as physical capability, physical capability cannot be counterbalanced very far by mental capability once combat is underway. This assumes, of course, that no weapons are used. When weapons are used, the individual combat advantage shifts from physical capability to mental capability. This assumes that the greater mentality will produce a better weapon and use it with greater skill. A better weapon example would be a spear over a club.

With the advantage in the establishment of control by means of individual combat shifted from physical capability to mental capability, the next step was logically to shift the means of the establishment of control away from individual combat entirely. This shift could be particularly desirable for the more intelligent controllers as they became older and less physically capable. Whether this shift was created by man or evolved because of the original increased benefit to the group, is immaterial. The result was the development of two different means for the establishment and maintenance of a controller-controlled relationship without any physical involvement by the controller. The first means was based on psychological fear and the second was based on trade.

Since fear of failure in combat was most likely the original deterrent to the challenge of leadership, the next logical step was for a controller to establish a means of shifting the fear of the controlled from the fear of failure in combat to fear of combat with the controller. To do this the controller must create in the minds of the controlled the fear of retribution should the controller be defeated in combat or harmed in any way. But to carry out the retribution would require one or more individuals who were in between the controller and the controlled status. Also to establish these in between individuals as a legitimate means of retribution upon the controlled, the controller would have to give them something in return for their promised retribution services. He would have to control them by trade rather than by fear. With this arrangement the controller could tell the controlled that if anyone were to harm him his men would kill them.

The next step, of course, would be for the controller's men to control the controlled with the authority of the controller. Then the controller's men would establish their men to add another step in the chain of control. As each level of control would be established, the controller would become more isolated and more secure from the controlled, but less secure from overthrow within his control establishment.

To what extent and to what complexity this human means of control progressed before it became interspersed with control by means of the fear of the supernatural is unknown. Some form of the supernatural seems to have been present in the earliest findings of recorded history and yet man must have developed a means of group control beyond individual combat before he developed the supernatural as a means of control.

To the early man, the supernatural must have been as obvious as the falseness of the supernatural should be today. To the early man, nothing would have had any logical or natural connection. Nothing would have made sense. Water would fall from nowhere in a sky that went straight up to those little bright spots. The temperature would get hot and then cold for no reason at all. Then the air would move faster and faster and the sky would flash and crash and the ground would shake and animals and people would die. Sometimes game would be plentiful and sometimes it would just disappear and everything would turn brown and dry. Sometimes whole forests would burn. Sometimes almost everyone would just die without even being hurt. It must have been quite obvious to the early man that somewhere, somehow, there was something he couldn't see that was after him from time to time. With an unseen power as great as this around, what could have been more natural than the use of this power as a means of control. The use of the fear of this apparently supernatural power as a means of control must have been as natural as the use of wood to float a raft on water without any idea of why it floated. This unseen power could be used by the early controller in the same way as his men. It could be used as the threat of retribution. It was sure to strike sooner or later.

The Three Party System

The three parties in this system are:
1. The controlled
2. The controller
3. The imaginary unapproachable authority

In this system the controller (2) plays the roll of interpreter and spokesman for the unapproachable authority (3). The controller never claims to be the originator of the dictates of the authority. Therefore, the controlled (1) can never question the authority directly. The controlled cannot question the authority of the controller since the controller claims no authority. The controlled can question the authority through the controller, but since the authority is imaginary, this is futile.

The imaginary unapproachable authority is backed by some form of fear. Disregard for the authority or disobedience of the dictates of the authority brings punishment. The punishment may take many forms. When the system is instilled as a belief in childhood, the punishment is in the form of a guilt complex and a fear of a horrible unknown retribution in the future. Since most men have occasional disasters, these become convincing punishment. Further, there is the fear of a possible horrible unknown punishment after death. Finally there is the fear of ostracism. The various possibilities of this punishment were at one time one of the major art forms of the Christian religion. See Hieronymus Bosch 1450-1516 Flanders; Pieter Brueghel 1525-1569.

To prevent punishment, the controller prescribes complete self-demeaning, self-belittling worship or adoration of the authority. This prescription supposedly pleases the authority by increasing the contrast between the self-demeaning controlled and the all powerful authority. An important attribute of this prescription is that the controlled who are self-demeaning, self-belittling, worshipful and adoring of authority are much more readily controlled and much less likely to question.

The "Three Party System" works. It can be used by an individual or an "in" group of individuals to subjugate and control men's minds. This applies from the primitive witch doctor to the most powerful world religions and governments. It applies to many types of societies and businesses, particularly large corporations.

The results of the control of men's minds through the use of the "Three Party System" may be only restrictive and thwart progress or it may be very bad and create war. For thousands of years the Egyptians used this system to control the populace without the need of a police force. The imaginary unapproachable authority rested in the gods. The controllers were the priests and the dictates came from the ruling family who were the living representatives of the gods. The populace was convinced that every act was witnessed by one or another of a multitude of gods. Unlawful or immoral acts were punished by subsequent difficulties or natural disasters such as pestilence, disease, famine and death. Since the system of gods, morals and laws was complex, there was no way to keep from doing some kind of act undesirable to the gods. Therefore, the populace was always prepared for the natural disasters which were bound to take place. However, since the populace was convinced that these disasters were caused by their own wrong doing, they were constantly striving to abide by the laws and to do as they were told to prevent further or future disaster.

Mankind has evolved as a social animal under a system of controlled and controllers. Seldom have controllers attempted to control alone without the backup of an imaginary unapproachable authority. The use of this imaginary backup authority by the controllers has divided mankind against itself.

Mankind is one species distinct in many remarkable ways from other animals. However, one sad distinction is that no other specie of higher animal is divided against itself for the purpose of mass self destruction. Admittedly this would be difficult for a higher animal other than man, using only the teeth.

Mankind would never have spent almost the whole of recorded history in the attempted destruction of his own kind if he believed this to be wrong and could control his own destiny. He would not have done so because other men requested him to. He had to be convinced of the righteousness of war. He had to be convinced that some power above and beyond the power of men, wished him to destroy his own kind. He had to be convinced that he would receive some reward beyond that which his immediate associates could give him. He had to fear retaliation and ostracism if he refused to comply with the authority and agree to kill his own kind. This imaginary power has been his gods and his patriotism for his state. With these two backup powers, controllers have caused the controlled of different imaginary gods or different imaginary symbolic representations of social groups to try enmass to destroy each other.

Thus, a reasonable supposition is that rational men will not destroy each other enmass for personal reasons or because other men tell them they must. Rational men must be made to feel that the large scale destruction of other men is righteous. Controllers could not readily create war without third party backing. There is no recorded instance of this having happened. The truth is that controllers always have and now are using the "Three Party System," to divide mankind against itself to create war for the purpose of expanding their control.

The "Three Party System" is firmly stamped in the minds of all men. It is the essence of all social control. To speak against the "Three Party System" is to speak against the essence of all social control. To speak thus against an established system of social control has always been called heresy and treason. Most of today's systems of social control were once heresy and treason even though they are simply variations in the "Three Party System."

To speak the truth about the fallacy of the "Three Party System" and thus attack the essence of all social control is justified as an information background for the proposal of a new essence of all social control. The proposed new essence of all social control is composed of the truth of the present system. It is the present system stripped of the false third party.

Does the stripping away of falseness and the maintenance of residual truth constitute heresy and treason? It always has in the past. That has been the basis for the maintenance of the "Three Party System."

However, there is no way to establish a Two Party System without doing away with a Three Party System and for the eventual preservation of humanity, we must establish a Two Party System.

The three party system as used today for the control of men's minds is certainly working just as it has always worked. However, the recent rapid accumulation of physical truth seems to be creating a questioning attitude in all fields including education, politics, law, and business management. This questioning attitude, if expanded, could affect the functioning of the "Three Party System." For the three party system to function requires that the controlled not know that the unapproachable authority is imaginary. If the controlled realized the imaginary nature of the unapproachable authority, they might realize that they were dealing with the human authority of the controllers themselves. Such authority can be based on human judgement only. The controlled would realize that humans judgement can be in error and, therefore, the questioning of such judgment would not be futile. Human authority could still invoke reprisal for acts against the authority. But the controlled would know that the reprisal was instigated by the will of the controllers and not the imaginary unapproachable authority. The controlled could hold the controllers responsible and the controllers would, for the first time, have to accept personal responsibility for the results of their use of authority. The controllers would, for the first time, be personally responsible and accountable to the controlled. This concept will be called the "Two Party System."

The Two Party System

The two parties in this system are:
1. The controlled
2. The controllers

In this system the controllers would have to control based on some advantage returned to at least some part of the controlled. Even a tyrant must return advantage to those who keep him in control. But, with the "Two Party System", those required to keep the controllers in control must be a much larger percentage of the controlled than with the "Three Party System."

The requirement for the controllers to accept personal responsibility and accountability for the results of the use of authority would tend to establish control in those who returned the greatest advantage to the largest percentage of the controlled. For the controllers to fail to return an adequate advantage to a suitable percentage of controlled would result in a revolt or a lost election which is a rather peaceful revolt.

Thus, the controllers do not arbitrarily have authority except as it is given to them by the controlled. This must have been what some of the writers of the United States Constitution had in mind when they tried to establish a "Two Party System" of controllers and controlled separate from any imaginary unapproachable authority. However they failed.

To the extent that the controllers have convinced the controlled of the existence of an imaginary unapproachable third party called the state or union or society as a whole or the U.S. Government or the Soviet Socialist Republic, or any religion, to this extent the controllers are no longer accountable to the controlled. Wherever a controller claims his authority rests anywhere other than in himself with the consent of the controlled, there exists a "Three Party System."

The armed forces of most countries represent typical three party systems. Here, the final authority rests in the imaginary third party called the State. The State is generally represented by an idol called a flag which men prostrate before or salute or die for. Here the controllers do not accept any personal accountability to the controlled for the results of the use of authority. Their accountability is only to the imaginary State from whence comes their authority. On this basis the controllers can order their controlled to death with no compunction.

Only in an armed forces version of the "Three party System" could the controllers maintain control since there is no incentive to return any advantage to the controlled except as self defense. However, to make control simpler, there is generally some system of medals and honors and privilege to placate the lack of advantage to the controlled.

In some countries the third party concept of a state as a final unapproachable authority is so powerful that the controllers go so far as to draft some of the controlled into the armed forces against their will to wage non-defensive war in foreign countries. Under this system it seems to be easier to rationalize the draft of part of the controlled for purposes of killing and destroying than for useful purposes of construction or farming or manufacturing. The latter would be called slavery.

Some businesses succeed in establishing three party systems to control employees. Wherever the management strongly stresses company loyalty or makes decisions backed by a statement that it is company policy where such policy has not been previously written, understood, and agreed to, the management is trying to derive authority from an imaginary entity. The words company and corporate are expressions of business concepts, they have no existence in themselves. There is only a building with some equipment occupied by some controllers and some controlled. Into the building comes some material and out of the building goes the same material in a different form. Into the building comes some blank paper and some printed paper and out of the building goes some printed paper and some paper trash. Into the building comes some money and out of the building goes the same money. That is all there is to any business. There may be less but there is never more. This then is a method, a procedure, a concept. It is nothing which can require loyalty or from which authority can be derived. On the other hand, if a controller says I require loyalty, if he says I establish a policy as follows etc., —, then he himself is responsible and he must accept accountability. Now a "Two party System" exists. If his policies are good and if the company and the employees prosper, he will get the loyalty he desires. Only when he uses a non-existent third party, called the company, as the source of his authority does a controller utilize the "Three Party System."

With the "Two Party System" the controlled can hold the controllers, the second party, accountable for the success of their control just as controllers hold the controlled accountable for carrying out their assignments.

With the "Three Party System" the controlled cannot hold the controllers, the second party, accountable for the success of their control since the controllers disclaim personal accountability. The controlled cannot hold the imaginary third party accountable since it is non-existent. This results in control by authority without accountability.

Will the Two Party System Suffice

Is the "Three Party System" necessary or will the "Two Party System" suffice?

By definition the three party system is based on the false premise of the existence of a non-existent third party. Yet a large part of humanity will remain convinced of the existence of about any third party which any controllers wish to utilize. Another large part of humanity will recognize the non-existence of any third party but they will rationalize the use of the third party as necessary to maintain control. Strangely enough, many controllers seem to convince themselves of the actual existence of a third party. Still more strangely; many controlled, who realize the non-existence of a third party, rationalize the need for one. They actually accept a known non-existent third party as the authority for the dictates of their controller.

With this strange psychological reaction by a large part of humanity, there is bound to be a strong and perhaps overwhelming belief by both controllers and controlled that the "Three Party System" is necessary. There will be much argument that the three party system is wrong here but right there. Wrong when used by some controllers for some purposes but right for others.

The origin of any "Three Party System" is based on intentional deception by falsehood for the purpose of control by would be controllers. Even if the achievement of control thus gained is apparently good, if deception and falsehood are considered necessary to control, then what is the value of truth and how is humanity to build a moral code based on truth with deception and falsehood as its foundation? How can the end justify the means when the purpose of the end is truth and the means to the end is falsehood?

Truth exists and wherever it has been found, mankind has been able to live with it and to gain from it.

Untruth and deception are spoken and written and believed but they do not exist. Mankind has been able to live amidst untruth and deception but has never gained from it.

Throughout recorded history man has lived for the most part under various forms of the "Three Party System." There have been and are now various forms of the "Two Party System." The "Two Party System" is functional. Therefore, I would propose that the "Two Party System" would suffice but that a moral code based on truth to determine good and bad would be required to replace the present moral code. I speculate that a transition of mankind to the "Two Party System" with an appropriate moral code would be lengthy and difficult. I would speculate that several generations might be required because of the psychological fear inherent in the "Three Party System" which is engendered by most educational systems from generation to generation.

The "Three Party System" and associated moral codes has not and cannot produce an efficient, creative, productive and peaceful world society. The "Two Party System" and an associated moral code based on truth to determine good and bad should produce an efficient, creative, productive and peaceful world society.

The Efficiency and Productivity of the "Two Party System"

With little fanfare and perhaps unknowingly, industrial management has been evolving rapidly toward a form of "Two Party System."

This evolution follows the principle of the "Survival of the Fittest," in the business world. This form of "Two Party System" has begun to evolve because of the great increase in efficiency which results. The industrial terminology which applies to this form of "Two Party System" is:

Responsibility - responsibility must be given authority

Authority - authority must be held accountable

Accountability - accountability is to those who give responsibility

A chief executive of any corporation is held accountable to the stockholders through the directors who give him the responsibility and authority to control the corporation so long as they are satisfied. When the stockholders are unsatisfied they can go to the directors at a stockholder meeting or sell their stock or both. Thus management (specifically chief executive or controller) is responsible for a competitive profit. Management has the authority to produce a competitive profit and is held accountable for a competitive profit.

The employees and particularly the union employees, hold industrial management accountable for operating the business in such a way that the employees can be paid a competitive wage. When the employees are unsatisfied, they strike or quit or both. Thus management is accountable for competitive wages.

The customers and even the government hold industrial management responsible for a suitably competitive product. When the customers are unsatisfied they become non customers. When the government becomes unsatisfied, the industry may come to a halt by injunction.

Thus, industrial management (particularly the chief executive or controller) has an accountability for:

competitive products

competitive wages

competitive return to stockholders.

If industrial management fails to adequately satisfy these accountabilities, the management is replaced with hopefully more capable controllers. If the interval selection and replacement process fails over a long enough period of time, the corporation will become bankrupt. In this case new controllers are appointed by an external process.

In none of these accountabilities is the corporate management able to rely on a third party to maintain control if accountability is not satisfied. Since industrial management cannot rely on a third party to maintain themselves in power if they fail to satisfy their accountabilities, the control of corporate management is a form of "Two Party System." This form of "Two Party System" is not according to definition because industrial management is not directly accountable to the controlled alone - the employees. Therefore, industrial management sometimes uses the "Three Party System" to control the employees directly. While the "Three Party System" is very effective as a means of employee control, it is ineffective in producing an efficient operation. Therefore, if free competition exists, evolution will reduce the use of the, "Three Party System" in the industrial management of employees.

Thus, in this form of "Two Party System," industrial management accountability is to the controllers of industrial management and not to the employees who are controlled by industrial management as in the definition of "Two Party System." But who are the customers, the wage earners and the stockholders of corporations. To a great extent they are those who are controlled by some industrial management or other stockholders such as those of insurance and the various funds. In no case can these controllers of industrial management effectively employ a, "Three Party System" form of employee control.

This concept of corporate management direct accountability with no third party backup has made business management develop into more and more of a science even though a fuzzy science. The necessity of selecting new controllers when accountability has not been satisfied has tended to place the most capable business scientists in control. This development has greatly increased the efficiency and the creativity of business management. Businesses which have not utilized controllers who were business scientists and capable of extremely efficient business operations no longer exist. This is evolution at work.

With the newly developed sophistication of business science, all business is subject to the natural laws of evolution. With evolution, the delicate balance which keeps any business in operation is easily upset. A few simple unbalancing upsets which can throw a business out of existence are as follows:

Competitive Products:

A new product which has unforeseen performance, quality or market problems which create customer resentment.

A new proprietary competitive product which cannot be matched.

Competitive Wages:

Inadequate payment of wages which results in loss of key management people.

Excessive wages without increased performance which results in loss of profit position.

Competitive Return to Stockholders:

Inadequate external return will result in lack of external capital availability for continued long range operation.

Excessive internal return will result in a lack of internal capital availability for continued long range profitable operation.

If caught in time, many unbalancing industrial forces which are from internal sources, can be understood and corrected by a change which may involve changed controllers. Many unbalancing industrial forces are from external sources and can be corrected if understood and caught in time. However, some external unbalancing forces cannot be corrected even though perfectly understood and completely foreseen. Since no correction is possible, the scientific management solution is diversification of industry so that the part affected by the incorrectable unbalancing force can be abandoned without disastrous effects to the corporation. The examples of these abandoned operations caused by incorrectable external unbalanced forces are as follows:

The replacement of the ice man.

Computers to replace mechanical business machines.

The industrial moves to the south to replace non-competitive operations in the northeast.

Jet engine operations to replace radial reciprocating engine operations.

Tape cassettes to replace record players to C.D.'s

The industrialization of housing to replace the building trades.

None of these types of evolutions happen overnight; all are foreseeable; many are in process; all improve operating efficiency.

The improvement in efficiency which results when "Two Party System" control replaces "Three Party System" control, is an improvement in the efficiency of the operation controlled - not an improvement in the efficiency of control itself. Control through the "Two Party System" is much more difficult and requires much more effort than control through the "Three Party System." Therefore, controllers will use the "Two Party System" when they must to survive competitive operations with "Two Party System" control. Controllers will use the "Two Party System" when they understand the potential for improved operational efficiency, to reinforce and expand their sphere of control. Controllers will use the "Two Party System" when the controlled become adequately informed to refuse to accept a third party.

The improved efficiency of operation which results from holding controllers personally accountable for satisfactory performance is derived from controller's fear of loosing control. To produce satisfactory results, a controller must now use all of his energy and his creative ability since he cannot rely on a third party. Further, he must inspire his controlled to do likewise.

Thus, the "Two Party System" increases operational efficiency by both the natural selection of the most capable controllers and by forcing controllers to operate to their utmost capability.

Chapter 18
Freedom and Achievement

The meaning of freedom will be considered only as the state of being free with respect to man. The meaning of free will be considered only as:

    free to --- socially uncontrolled not as

    free from --- without

The meaning of, "true freedom" for man will be --- absolutely uncontrolled. The meaning of, "individual freedom" for man will indicate the degree of freedom of one man with respect to other men.

Man has always existed with some degree of individual freedom and some degree of applied control or restraint. The control has been applied by his inherent ability, his physical environment and by his fellow man or his society. Even the most powerful controller must be controlled by his inherent ability and his informational background which is the product of his society. Beyond this, he is controlled by social rules with which he must comply to maintain such control as he has. Historical records of social systems will describe these social rules. While these social rules constitute the means of control, they also constitute the restrictions of a controllers freedom. A controller is not free to refrain from controlling if he wishes to continue to control.

All human achievement is controlled by rules. First, of course, the achievement must be within the rules dictated by natural laws. Next, the achievement most likely must be controlled by social rules. If the social rules are such that they do not conflict with natural laws, then achievement may take place. However, social rules may often conflict with natural laws and prevent achievement. Social rules may also determine whether a specific achievement may or may not be attempted. For instance, only the ruling class were allowed to learn to read in most medieval societies. By the same social rule certain of the ruling class were not free to refrain from learning to read.

All human achievement is mental or physical or a combination of mental and physical. Mental achievement is limited to all forms of thought and all forms of communication of such thought. Mental achievement has generally been controlled by somewhat different social rules from those applied to achievement which involves physical action. Only social rules for physical achievement are imperative for social control. Social rules for the control of mental achievement may be applied to restrain potential physical achievement but so long as physical achievement adverse to the society is controlled, social rules for the control of mental achievement are not imperative to social control.

All human societies are composed of individuals who achieve within the limits of the following general conditions of freedom:

1. The controlled use of natural laws.
2. Various kinds and degrees of physical environmental control.
3. Various inherent mental and physical abilities.
4. Various informational backgrounds.
5. Various kinds and degrees of social controller responsibilities.
6. Various kinds and degrees of applied social control.

These general conditions reveal that "true freedom" has many natural restraints as well as social restraints. Further, individual freedom would be restrained and relative even without the restraints of social control. Within these general conditions, any individual will have such individual freedom for mental and physical achievement as his peculiar condition permits.

Of the general conditions which limit human achievement, the first three are natural restraints and man can do very little to change them. Even though man cannot change these natural restraints, he is free to achieve within the limitations of these restraints unless restrained by the social controls of the last three general conditions. The last three general conditions which limit human achievement are imposed by man and can therefore be changed. These three general conditions determine the social control and, thereby, the individual freedom of achievement within any human society.

Within any human society, the balance of social control and the resulting individual freedom of mental and physical achievement will determine the moral and material progress of the society.

Thus, freedom is the antithesis of control and neither freedom nor control are inherently right or wrong or good or bad. Rather the areas and the extent of the application of social controllers together with the areas and extent of the resulting individual freedom to achieve determines the capability of the society. The better the capability of the society, the better was the balance which generated the capability.

The Battle of the Systems

Of all social controls, individual freedom balances; the one least likely to produce increased capability of a society is the social control of mental achievement.

Innumerable rationalizations can be made for the maintenance of the "Three Party System" of national political control and the squelching of the "Two Party System." The foremost rationalization will be the requirement of the "Three Party System" as the only means to maintain an armed defense of the "Free World" against the "Unfree World." Both the "Free World" and the "Unfree World" feel forced to use the "Three Party System" in an aggressive manner to try to overcome each other. This is the rationalization of fear and is based on the premise that only through defensive war preparation, which at times may seem aggressive in nature, can either the "Free World" or "Unfree World" defend itself. While the controllers of most social systems base their continued control on the use of the "Three Party System," the results of their control must produce some benefit for a suitable percentage of the controlled. The higher the percentage and the greater the material satisfaction of the controlled, the more internally secure is the position of the controllers. The more internally secure the controllers become the less reason they have to risk loss of control through external aggression and the less reason they have to suppress individual freedom of expression.

While the "Free World" produces more material goods than the "Unfree World" and, therefore, should have a higher percentage of satisfied controlled, there still is a tendency on the part of the "Free World" controllers to try to restrict individual freedom when control problems are encountered.

The "Unfree World" has produced an increasing amount of material goods but not yet comparable to that produced by the "Free World." Still as the "Unfree World" controlled have been slightly more satisfied, their individual freedom has increased ever so slightly. The controllers seem to be much more fearful of their controlled than they are of external controller aggression.

However, their concern for external controller aggression is so materially expensive to satisfy that the material goods increase available to the controlled remains small and unsatisfying. If the controlled of the Unfree World were materially more satisfied than the controlled of the Free World, the Unfree World controllers should feel secure from internal overthrow. With no fear of internal overthrow there need be no fear of internal personal freedom. With internal personal freedom, the Unfree World would not be unfree.

This war preparation is not the only defense against a competing "Three Party System" for social control. In fact, war preparation is a very poor defense compared to the economic defense possible with the "Two Party System." A society with political, industrial and moral "Two Party System" control even partially operational would begin to operate extremely efficiently. It would rapidly become so materially (economically) powerful because of increased efficiency that the "Unfree World" controllers using the "Three Party System" could no longer compete or retain control except through informational isolation. Otherwise they would logically be forced toward the "Two Party System." As the Unfree World control system changed and as material improvement took place, the reason for fear of external overthrow would disappear. Without fear of internal controllers, there would be no reason for controllers to restrain the personal freedom of the controlled. With material abundance in both worlds and freedom of the controlled in both worlds there would be little incentive the controllers of either world could use to incite the controlled to war.

There is no logical reason for war to occur between social groups which are controlled by systems which provide material abundance to the satisfaction of the controlled and, therefore, individual freedom of thought and expression.

There is logical reason for war to occur between social groups which are controlled by systems which squander their material resources on war preparation and thereby must deprive the unsatisfied controlled of freedom of thought and expression to retain control.

There is less logical reason for war to occur between a social group which is controlled by a system which provides material abundance to the satisfaction of the controlled and, therefore, individual freedom—and a social group which is controlled by a system which squanders its material on war and thereby must deprive the unsatisfied controlled of freedom of thought and expression to retain control—provided free commerce and some informational exchange takes place. Under this condition the social group control system which supplies the greatest material abundance and freedom of thought and expression to its controlled should diffuse the means of this performance into the social group control system which supplies the least to its controlled. This diffusion should take place by natural selection and the survival of the fittest. This diffusion seems to be taking place between the free and unfree industrial world now to some extent.

The next rationalization might be that the controllers of a society which has become internally very efficient and very satisfied through "Two Party System" control, will have no fear of internal overthrow and, therefore, feel perfectly free to expand their control by external aggression. If the external aggression is economic, the possibility is logical. If the external aggression is by war, the possibility does not exist. Aggressive war offers satisfaction only to controllers, not to the satisfied controlled. Without a third party there is no way to offer satisfaction to the controlled through aggressive war. A "Two Party System" controller who attempts aggressive war, sparks immediate dissatisfaction among the controlled and thereby does himself in.

Another rationalization might be that an operationally efficient

"Two Party System" controlled society with its satisfied controlled would be a "sitting duck" for an externally aggressive operationally inefficient ""Three Party System" controlled society with its unsatisfied controlled. Such a rationalization would seem justified if there were no free trade or informational interchange between the two societies and if the "Three Party System" society were much better armed. However, no such condition exists or is likely to exist. First, trade and informational interchange between most societies is increased. Second, a "Two Party System" could only evolve in a highly technical society with a high educational capability. Third, the conversion to a "Two Party System" would require much time so that a society would not be defenseless while becoming more and more materially powerful through rapid technological advancement. Technological advancement is the only means of increased material power. With rapid material and technological advancement, some means must be found to help the aggressive "Three Party System" controlled society to improve materially. To help such a society improve is a much more logical defense than to isolate and maintain an ever expanded armed defense against such a society. To isolate and maintain an armed defense is to prevent the establishment of a "Two Party System." The "Two Party System" controller cannot rely on the third party necessary for war. Rather he must rely on scientific management to create material conditions through technological advances which make the requirement for war non-existent. For the "Two Party System" war should consist of material and technological assistance to aggressors. An adequate amount of this kind of war will overthrow the "Three Party System" of any aggressor and establish individual freedom in any society

A Real Third Party

Almost all of humanity is to some extent both controller and controlled. Probably all humans are controlled by others in some manner and to some extent; however, there may be some adults who are generally controllers of no one. Almost always the control is by some form of the "Three Party System" either expressed or implied. The third party of previous discussions has been imaginary and therefore unavailable. However, the third party may be real. While the third party is not always imaginary, the third party is always unavailable and capable of retribution. This unavailability may be only temporary or only difficult to overcome. The capability of retribution may be true or imagined. Examples of the simple use of a real, unavailable third party:

A mother says to a child, "Stop playing and study or your father will punish you when he comes home."

A wife says to her husband, "Slow down or you will be arrested for speeding."

A teacher says to a pupil, "Stop talking in class or you will be sent to the principal."

The mother thinks the use of the third party is more effective or less effort than an explanation of the advantage of study over continued play. The child can argue with the explanation but not with his father who isn't there.

The wife thinks the use of the third party is more effective than an explanation of her concern over the danger of excessive speed. The husband can argue with his wife's concern but he is not sure about a police car in the area and he cannot argue with a posted speed limit.

The teacher thinks the use of the third party is more effective than an explanation of the selfishness of an unauthorized class disruption by an individual. The pupil can argue the point with the teacher but the principal isn't there.

In these three simple cases there is an attempt to control minds by the establishment of a controller and controlled relationship. The controller does not offer to return any advantage to the controlled as in the "Two Party System." The controller offers only the threat of retribution by an unavailable but real third party if control is not accepted. In all cases the real third party can eventually be confronted. Therefore, the effectiveness of this form of "Three Party System" depends on the real or imagined power of retribution of the real third party compared to that of an imaginary third party. Generally an imaginary third party can be made much more effective provided the controlled can be prevented from questioning the imaginary third party's existence.

Chapter 19
Human Ability

A concept of human ability must be established to understand the society of humans or any part of humanity. Humans are what their ability allows them to be under the circumstances of their existence.

Humanity is as varied as its number. Perhaps two electrons are alike; two protons or perhaps even two neutrons may be alike. Even here, there may be no alikeness but only very very close similarity. Above this size range, differences from particle to particle are detectable by test. Therefore all life forms are unalike. They may be quite similar in many respects but they are never alike or equal.

Human ability can be demonstrated by almost purely physical achievement or purely mental achievement or by achievement requiring various combinations and amounts of physical and mental ability.

The achievement of human ability can be demonstrated to be helpful or harmful to an individual or their associates. It may be helpful to some and harmful to others. The achievement of human ability is great or small without regard to whether it is helpful or harmful.

To consider the physical and mental aspects of human ability, a reasonable definition would be that all mental activity takes place in a brain and that no appreciable physical activity takes place there. A further definition would be that all physical activity takes place outside a brain and that no mental activity takes place there. Thus, by definition, mental activity is by brain and physical activity is by every other part of a body.

Both a brain and its body function voluntarily and involuntarily. However, the body cannot function voluntarily except when so instructed by a brain. Thus, a brain voluntarily controls all human action and reaction including involuntary bodily action. Even though a brain controls a body as though a body were simply a sensing transmitting and material handling means for a brain, still a body is constituted in such a way that its normal electrochemical activity creates signals recognizable to a brain as impetus to instruct the body in certain physical pursuits which are necessary for the physical preservation of the body. These bodily signals urge a brain to create physical activity which results in supplying the body with food, water, oxygen, temperature control, sex and rest. While the body urges a brain to create these physical activities, a brain can overcome these urges and refrain from instructing the body in such physical activity.

A brain has some very remarkable known abilities. It probably has some even more remarkable unknown abilities. However, as remarkable as brains may be, they are all very very imperfect and limited in their ability to think. Of course, some brains are very poor and can hardly think at all, but the majority of brains can think fairly well in some categories. Some brains can think extremely well in some categories and fairly well in others. Apparently no brains can think extremely well in all categories. To discuss brains and bodies in the sense that brains have bodies and bodies do NOT have brains is very difficult because the English language is based on the false concept that you and I are bodies who have brains. Actually, we are brains who have bodies and there is no standard way to say this in English.

To say that a human thinks is to say that they are a brain who thinks. There is nothing about a human which can tell a brain to think. There is nothing about a human which has or receives or transmit any intelligence at all except a brain. Thus, the things we are used to thinking of as people are really only sensors, transmitters, energy converters, reproducers and material handlers. The controlling people who are ourselves and other people are brains. When we say, "I will do this or that," we mean we a brain will control our body to do it. When we say, "I'll think about it," we mean we a brain has sent a message to us to rummage through our memory and hook together whatever seems pertinent and come back with some conscious sense.

When I say, "my brain," I give the impression to others and to myself that I am a person who has a brain. I am giving the impression that the person who I am is my body. That my body can of its own volition conceive and speak possessively of the brain which controls it. Obviously this is not possible. Brains knowingly possess bodies but bodies cannot knowingly possess brains.

To realize that there is no I except a brain is difficult. Nevertheless, this is true. Therefore, I don't have a brain, I am a brain or a brain is me which ever you prefer. This difficult realization may arise from our inability to see ourselves or each other as brains. We both see only our transmitting, receiving and material handling equipment or our bodies. Since a brain's body, until quite recently, has been considered to be the person himself, a change in the identity of a person from a visible body to a hidden brain is difficult.

Since a person is a brain and a brain's body consists of its sensors, transmitters, energy convertor, reproducer and material handler, the pronouns variations of he and she should be reserved for male and female brains and it for his and her body.

The mental ability of a brain can be divided into categories. One category will be a brains ability to skillfully control the brain's body for various physical achievements. To a great extent, the skill of a brain's bodies physical achievements will depend upon the quality of the brain's body. To skillfully achieve physically, requires the inheritance of a body potentially suitable to the particular physical achievement and the development of the body for the achievement by a brain capable of managing such development. To the extent that these requirements are lacking, the degree of skill in the achievement will be lacking.

Another mental ability category is memory. Almost all brains have this ability to a varied degree and in various forms. The potential limit of this ability is established at birth and varies greatly. The development of this ability is a function of environment and time. The memory ability consists of two processes. One process consists of getting information into a brain's memory and the other process consists of getting the information back out of a brain's memory and in a conscious form. The first process is perception and the second is recall.

The degree of memory ability at a particular time might be determined by the percent of the perceived information consciously stored which can be recalled. This determination might be defined by the determination of the speed with which information can be recalled. It might be further defined by an analysis of the recall based on the time in storage. Under this sort of memory ability determination, different brains would yield all sorts of different forms of capabilities. Some would have a high percent of rapid recall for a short time period and then a rapid decline. Some would have a low percent of rapid recall but a high percent of slow recall for a long time period. All would have a higher percent of recall in some information categories than in others.

If a brain's memory process is somewhat like a computer's, then it is fairly well understood. If this is so then brains must have very poor processors, very poor memory circuitry for some kinds of information and no protection against occasionally losing contact with some memory banks. Actually, brains don't seem to function at all like computers and that is very fortunate.

While memory ability is very desirable, it should not be confused with thinking ability. Thinking requires memory but memory does not necessarily require much thinking.

The mental ability to think is as diverse as the number of brains. Thought ability potential, like memory ability potential, is chemically limited at birth. Neither the memory process nor the thought process is well understood. What takes place is known to some extent but how it takes place is not well known. Brains have the ability to think but since brains are the controllers, there is nothing but themselves to tell them to think. They may not think without some primary outside stimulus. Perhaps once started by a primary stimulus, most subsequent thought is a continuation of previously interrupted thought. Then, only when again stimulated, are additional primary thought processes started. If this is true, then all thought is reaction to stimulus outside the brain. The important thing here is that there is no way for a brain to knowingly develop or improve its thinking ability. Outside stimulus can broaden the subject matter about which a brain thinks, but it will think about the additional subjects the same way it thought about the few. A brain cannot of its own volition think better. A brain may vary its thinking ability from time to time depending on the state of its health. Like most functions, frequent exercise should help.

The degree of thought ability at a particular time cannot be measured in the manner of memory ability. Most attempts to measure thought ability as in I.Q. tests, tend to measure memory for the most part or conscious thought at best. The thought ability of most value takes place subconsciously and with an uncontrollable time requirement. Since most all test determinations take place within a time framework, there is no test method to determine subconscious thought ability.

A brain will think subconsciously to satisfy conscious thought requirements if it has the ability and if it is requested to make an intentional effort to do so. The subconscious thought process may take hours, days or weeks but after some period of time, a response to the originating effort will come forth in conscious thought. Apparently, more than one subconscious thought process can take place in the same brain at the same time. Maybe subconscious thought processes take place during skips in conscious thought processes.

Not much more is known about the subconscious thought process than that it exists. The subconscious thought process is not used intentionally by a very high percentage of brains. The majority of brains do not know that such a thought process exists. The lack of knowledge of the subconscious thought process or the lack of its intentional use, does not mean that brains do not use the process. This is the thought process by which much of creativity takes place. The subconscious thought process capability is undoubtedly built right in to standard brains just like memory. However, the process may not work very well in many brains. A knowledge that the process capability exists may be required to use it intentionally. However, much creative subconscious thought took place before the concept of a subconscious thought capability was developed.

Thus, a human is a combination of mental and physical equipment wherein the mental equipment is the controller. Human ability is determined by the potential limit of the inherited quality of the equipment and the environmental effect on the development of the equipment within its potential limits. Therefore, there is nothing about a human to make him much better or worse than he turns out to be. A poor quality brain with a poor quality environment will most likely produce a poor quality human of very limited ability of any kind. The same poor brain and body developed in a good environment will most likely produce the same poor quality human of very limited ability of any kind. If a poor brain with a good body is developed in a good environment, the result may be a useful human suited to some kind of manual labor or boxing. A good quality brain with a good quality body developed in a good quality environment will most likely produce a good quality human of high ability in a few categories, average ability in many categories, and poor ability in only a few categories. A good quality brain with any quality body in a poor quality environment will most likely produce a criminal but may produce a human with some ability depending on the breaks in the environment. Therefore, environment is a factor in the development of human ability only to the extent of the inherited mental and physical potential for development. Likewise human ability is the product of inherited mental and physical potential only to the extent of the environmental potential for such development.

High inherited potential may expedite a change of environment toward one of greater potential. Without the environmental improvement, the high inherited potential is useless in the development of human ability.

Thus we are not all created equal nor do we have an equal environment in which to develop equally.

Human "Three Party System" vs "Human Two Party System"

The barrier of the "Three Party System" has until recently, kept humans from questioning and investigating their own thought processes. This "Three Party System" consists of:
1. The controlled body
2. The controller brain
3. The imaginary unapproachable authority called the soul

162

The soul is regarded as being immortal and is credited with the functions of thinking and willing and hence determining all behavior. (Webster) Here, as before, the controller plays the role of the interpreter and spokesman of the imaginary unapproachable authority the soul. The controller is not supposed to be the originator of the dictates of the authority. Therefore, the controller cannot be held accountable since the controller claims no authority. However, when the controller makes a mistake in his interpretation of the dictates of the imaginary unapproachable authority, the soul can never be found to take the blame and the controller and the controlled are left holding the bag. Thus, the concept of a human "Three Party System" has for centuries produced a society of confused psychotics who believed they were controlled by a soul which continually got them into social and moral trouble and was always nowhere to be found for help. Their only recourse has been to seek aid from a religious controller and thus to still another third party or a direct appeal to the religious third party or a psychiatrist.

The "Human Three Party System" is an inherent leveler of all mankind. For while bodies and brains may not have equal ability, who is to say that souls do not have equal ability. If souls have equal ability in spite of brain and body inequalities, then social and moral wrongs must be deliberate misdeeds of the soul. Since all souls have equal ability, they must have equal responsibility. Therefore, there can be standardized misdeeds, both social and moral. For standardized misdeeds done by standardized souls there can be standardized punishment. This concept makes control very simple and straight forward and easy to apply. It also keeps society in a constant state of psychotic confusion and deadly strife.

For man to question the non-existent presence of an imaginary third party called a soul would have required man to break the barrier. He, therefore, never considered that he was a brain and that as a brain, he made such decisions as were made. True, these decisions were a function of his total background and the surrounding circumstances at the time of decision. Nevertheless, to the extent of his participation, the decisions were his.

163

Thus in truth, there exists but a "Human Two Party System" which consists of:

1. The controlled body
2. The controller brain

The controller brain is He is She and He and She are the authority and are as responsible as their human ability permit them to be.

The "Human Two Party System" is a separator of all mankind into levels of ability in each of all categories of ability. For no two bodies and brains do have equal abilities in any category and each must be considered according to their ability. This concept is not simple and straight forward, for there can be no standardized misdeeds either social or moral and, therefore, there can be no standardized punishment. This concept makes control very difficult to apply. It also may help cure the psychosis and strife of society.

In the "Human Two Party System", a person's value is nothing simply because they exist. Without an imaginary soul, a person's mere existence leaves a person worthless except for their potential. For the same reason, a person of great ability and corresponding achievement has a value far greater than that of most humans.

Truth exists

Truth cannot be created

Truth must be found

A person is what they are compared to other people and they are no more or less by self proclamation, by the proclamation of others, by association, by color, or by location in the universe.

If mankind should become extinct, the speed of light would not change.

Humanity As It Is

The designs of religious and political systems of control and the designs of moral codes of relationships have never considered humanity as it is. These designs have considered instead, humanity as the systems designers would have it. The incompatibility of the systems and codes with humanity as it is, has been rationalized by the concept that the systems and codes are right and humanity as it is, is wrong and, therefore, humanity as it is, must change to fit the systems and codes. Since the systems and codes are ineffective for humanity as it is, and since humanity as it is, doesn't seem to change much, there has been a continual impasse.

Humanity as it is, ranges from the very poor quality, completely incapable to the moderately good quality, moderately capable. We can readily conceive of humans of far greater quality and capability than actually exist. However, there isn't anything about the humans which make up humanity, to indicate that humanity is about to change much in the near future except hopefully they will become better educated. They might read this book.

Since humanity as it is won't change, the designs of the religious and political systems of control and the designs of moral codes of relationships must change or humanity will remain in the impasse. Actually the systems and codes do gradually change and this change affects changes in humanity.

Humanity as it is, must logically be dealt with as it is. The only way to deal with humanity as it is, is truthfully. Truth is the one possibility which has never been considered as a solution to the impasse in which humanity finds itself. By truth, I mean the truth which is found to exist by the evaluation thought process carried to extreme in all directions. I do not mean false truth created by humans and accepted as truth by them without any evaluation thought process.

Truth exists
Truth cannot be created
Truth must be found

Chapter 20
Rules for Good and Bad as Benefit and Harm

There are no words to denote the opposite direction from a center point between benefit and harm as plus and minus denote opposite directions of amount from some mid point. Therefore, good and bad in this discussion will be limited to denote such meanings. With these meanings established, good and bad as an effect of existence on humanity is determined by humans only.

Existence, in itself, has nothing to do with good and bad. Existence is simply the relationships generated by natural laws when forces move mass through space in time according to natural laws, and a knowledge of existence is determined by finding truth. That which is not true, does not exist and any reference to that which is not true is therefore imaginary.

Plus and minus can refer to an amount or to a direction. Plus and minus have no significance until some rules are established as to plus and minus what and where is the mid point. Plus and minus can refer to more or less of something than a given amount. Plus and minus can refer to the direction of force, velocity, or acceleration as in pull or push or go or come. But all of these concepts of plus and minus are related to an arbitrary mid point and are, therefore, not absolute. There seems to be an absolute end to energy level at absolute zero below which there is no minus. Whether there is an absolute zero of any other category is interesting to ponder. Void perhaps would qualify if there is such. With respect to an absolute zero, plus and minus have no significance. Therefore, plus and minus must refer specifically to an arbitrary mid point which is not an absolute zero, to have significance.

Existence effects changes in forces and mass. These changes can be determined as neither good nor bad until some rules have been established which determine what change and to what extent this change is considered good, bad or neither. Since these rules must be established by humans, the establishment of the rules originates good and bad for whomever established the rules.

There can be as many sets of rules for good and bad as there are humans who establish the rules unless more than one human agrees to the same set of rules. If more than one human agrees to the same set of rules, the set of rules produces benefit and harm understandably to these humans. If a universal set of rules for good and bad to produce benefit and harm could be established, then all men could agree to the same set of rules. A "Universal Concept of Good and Bad" would have to be such that all humans would benefit with the concept and would be harmed without it. Under these conditions, what could be their point of disagreement?

The "A" and "B" Patterns of Existence

From astronomical observations, man is familiar with only a very small segment of existence in the universe. Whether the rest of existence has anything like the solar system and the earth, elsewhere remains to be found out. From personal observation, man is familiar with only a very small part of the existence which surrounds him on earth and of which he is. Yet there are some truths about the general pattern of existence which seem reliable within present knowledge.

General Truths of Life Energy —

1. All life forms utilize energy to live.
2. Most all animate life forms *must* utilize energy derived from other life forms to live.
3. Most all inanimate life forms *may* utilize energy derived from other life forms to live but some may not.

The requirement for the use of dead life forms as an energy source to maintain life does not seem very sophisticated for humans. However, until chemistry can replace farming, dead life forms, whether animate or inanimate, will have to suffice.

Animate life depends upon life energy for existence. Human

167

animate life is no exception. Therefore, without a supply of life energy, human existence can not continue. Humans, like all other animals, exist at the expense of other life forms, and humans are undoubtedly the most concerned of all life forms about continued existence of the life formes they require for life energy. For these life energy life forms to continue to exist seems to require a long succession of life form existence, each dependent upon a number of lesser life forms. On the bottom rung of this succession may be life forms which derive their energy completely from chemical reaction not related to other life forms.

The interdependence of life forms which determines the possibility of continued human existence, forms a part of the pattern of existence which surrounds and includes human.

General Truths of Life Ambient:

1. All animate life forms must have water and air or oxygen.
2. All life forms must remain in a fairly narrow temperature range to function.

In the solar system, these ambient conditions appear to be unusual. In the universe they may or may not be unusual. On earth, these ambient conditions have not always existed and there is no reason to believe they will always continue to exist. The ambient condition under which human life and associated life forms exist on earth seems very precarious. This ambient condition is a very small band compared to the wide band of possible known abient conditions which can exist on earth.

There may be conditions of existence completely inconceivable to man. Then again there may not exist living conditions beyond man's conception. The condition observable by man may represent that which is typical for all possible existence. No one knows.

The narrow band of ambient conditions suitable to human existence forms a part of a pattern of existence which surrounds and includes man.

General Truths of Natural Life Enemies:

1. Most life forms have natural enemies in the form of predators, parasites, disease organisms, poisonous substances, etc.
2. Most life forms have natural enemies in the form of exaggerated ambient conditions such as storms, heat, cold, drought, pollution, radiation, etc.

The natural life enemies of humans change just as existence changes humans and humans change existence. Thus there is always the possibility that change will bring a natural enemy which will cause the extinction of humanity. So far, humans have conquered a number of natural life enemies; but for every one conquered, several new life enemies have been found to exist.

The growing number and knowledge of natural life enemies to human existence forms apart of the pattern of existence which surrounds and includes man. So also does the need to conquer these natural life enemies form a part of the pattern of existence if humans are to continue to exist.

The summation of the patterns of existence which have been discussed will be called the "A" pattern.

The "A" pattern of existence encompasses:

The Truths of Life Energy
The Truths of Life Ambient
The Truths of Life Natural Enemies

Since man continues to exist in the face of these natural hazards to existence, there appears to be a human desire to continue human existence. To continue to overcome these natural hazards to existence would seem to require achievement enough to keep mankind occupied. However, the human development of the "Three Party System" has caused mankind to deviate from achievement to conquer his natural enemies. The development of the "three Party System" has allowed controllers to incite mankind to conquer man. Thus there is another group of truths.

General Truths of Life Human Enemies:

1. Most all life forms refrain from the destruction of their own species except humans.
2. Human life forms are incited to destroy their own species enmass by human controllers through the use of the "Three Party System."

To continue to exist, man must achieve with respect to "Life Energy," "Life Ambient," and "Life Natural Enemies." However, a man's existence depends on achievement with respect to "Life Human Enemies." "Life Human Enemies" can bring about the extinction of humanity.

Until a large enough percentage of mankind becomes mentally

169

capable of questioning without fear and therefore becomes aware of the "Three Party System" trap into which mankind has fallen, there will be a summary pattern of existence which will be called the "B" pattern as distinct from the pervious "A" pattern

The "B" pattern of existence encompasses:

The Truths of Life Energy

The Truths of Life Ambient

The Truths of Life Natural Enemies

The Truth of Life Human Enemies

The "A" pattern of existence will be considered the "Natural Pattern", since it is concerned with man's conquest of natural hazards only.

The "B" pattern of existence will survive as long as the "Three Party System." The "Three Party System" is imbedded in almost every social organization in existence. It will stay imbedded until humans become mentally capable or inspired or brave enough to question and reject any concept as truth without documentary evidence to establish its identity with truth through the evaluation through process carried to extremes in all directions. Until humans question and find for themselves "The Philosophy of Truth,"

Truth exists

Truth cannot be created

Truth must be found

they will be part of the "B" pattern of existence. Without the mental capability to use the evaluation though process carried to extremes in all directions, man cannot tell the difference between the truth which exists and the false truth which has been created by man. Even men with great mental capability have mental blocks created by engendered fear which thwarts their use of the evaluation through process in such areas as their religion, their social status or their patriotism for instance. To question and then use the evaluation thought process to the extremes in all directions, requires more courage than most men have.

Truths in Purpose and Rules for Achievement

Truth has nothing to do with the direction of achievement either in favor of humanity or against humanity. Thus achievement in accordance with the natural laws of existence can harm as well as benefit humanity.

Man can achieve in accordance with the natural laws of existence at the expense of either man or *nature* exclusive of man. Truth does not determine that which harms or benefits man.

Truth pertains only to that which exists. That which exists is composed of forces moving mass through space in time which generate physical characteristics which are interrelated by natural laws only. Therefore, a purpose for existence and rules to achieve that purpose, in itself, can have neither truth nor untruth.

A purpose is a statement of a direction of intent.

A rule is a prescribed sequential procedure.

Neither a purpose nor a rule has any physical existences. However, a purpose can be such that its achievement fits the pattern of existence so that it can be in accordance with truth. Likewise rules can be such that when they are followed, there is no conflict with natural laws. The rules are then in accordance with truth and achievement can take place.

All purposes and rules for achievement are created by man. In themselves they have neither truth nor untruth. They can be in accordance with truth so that their achievement will either benefit or harm humanity. They cannot be in accordance with untruth and to the benefit of man. If a purpose and the rules for achievement are not in accordance with truth, the rules are not in accordance with natural laws and cannot lead to the achievement of the purpose. They are imaginary.

There is nothing in the natural laws of existence which prevents the creation and acceptance of a purpose and rules to achieve that purpose which are in accordance with truth and when achieved result in the extinction of humanity. Many of the previous forms of life have become extinct and most likely many more will become extinct in the near future. Whether the human life form is among those to become extinct will be determined by man's ability to create purposes and rules to achieve those purposes which fit the pattern of continued existence.

A "Universal Concept of Good and Bad"

In the sense of the universe, the word "nature" is the central character of existence. In the sense of the universe, the meaning of both words includes man. There is no word to denote all of existence or nature that does not include man as a brain. Therefore, in this discussion, the word nature when underlined as "<u>nature</u>" will denote all of nature or existence *other* than man as a brain. Thus the word "nature" does include man's material handling, energy conversion, sensory system, etc.

Within the universe, man is constantly changed by existence and in turn man changes existence. Unless man's effort to change existence is in accordance with some concept of good and bad, all changes by man and by existence will be without regard to good or bad or benefit or harm for man. Thus if man is to be benefited rather than harmed from his effort to change existence, he must first determine that the success of his effort to change existence will produce a benefit and not harm. When man makes this determination, he determines what he believes to be good and bad. The result of his effort may actually produce harm rather than benefit. But so long as his intention was to produce a benefit rather than just a random change, his intention was to determine good and bad. If the result was harm rather than the benefit he expected, he might then change his concept of good and bad and try again. On the other hand, he might misinterpret the result as a benefit where it was actually harmful or neither harmful nor beneficial. In this case he might not change his concept of good and bad even though it was in error. Thus, by cut and try, man can establish rules which govern his effort to change existence to produce what he believes will result in benefit rather than harm.

When a cut and try process fails to change existence to produce a benefit, man sometimes tries to bypass nature and produce a benefit by means of the supernatural. Thus, man also establishes rules which govern his effort to change existence to produce a benefit by means of the supernatural.

All of these rules become a record of what man has determined will change existence to produce benefits and not harm. The record becomes a concept of good and bad.

If each man were to start from scratch to establish his own record or concept of good and bad, mankind would never progress very far. Each man would have established a different concept of good and bad based on the results of his particular cut and try efforts. To progress, man has found it beneficial to hand down the record, or concept of good and bad from generation to generation. Each generation may or may not make changes or additions to the record.

Unfortunately many of each older generation develop a tendency to perpetuate the status quo. The purpose is to use the record to control the younger generation and thereby to make the younger generation a duplicate of the older generation. In this way the older generation apparently hopes to perpetuate itself. Thus the older generation generally resents any changes or additions to the record which might jeopardize their perpetuity.

Since existence is constantly changing man, the younger generation must generally make some changes with respect to existence in spite of the older generation. However, the non-existent supernatural has no changing affect on man. Therefore, there is less natural impetus to make any changes in the record with respect to the supernatural. Therefore, the part of the record which pertains to the supernatural, changes much more slowly.

Since the record is the result of cut and try in nature and appeals to the supernatural in religion, after many generations of men in all of the parts of the earth, where various groups of men have congregated, the accumulated records are somewhat different. This has resulted in each group having somewhat different concepts of good and bad.

The number of the various groups would be reducing because of improved communications and transportation if it were not for the population explosion. If the number of groups reduced by communication and thereby natural selection of concepts, which produced the greatest benefit and the lease harm, a "Universal Concept of Good and Bad" might evolve. However, mankind may not last long enough for the evolutionary process to reduce the number of groups to one. This is particularly true since the difference in the records of the various groups is one of the principle reasons controllers are able to keep the groups separated.

If a "Universal Concept of Good and Bad" could b conceived which all groups could eventually accept, then the principle reason for the segregation would disappear. If such a concept were available and did exist, the controllers of each group would prevent its acceptance by the controlled as long as the controllers could maintain the "Three Party System."

To merit acceptance, a "Universal Concept of Good and Bad" must yield a greater benefit and less harm to all men than their present concept. Since any concept must be determined by man, man has but to determine such a concept. To yield a greater benefit to all men than their present concept of good and bad, a "Universal Concept" must be in accordance with:

1. The truth which exists
2. The Two Party System
3. Human Ability and the Nature of Achievement
4. The Human Two Party System
5. The "A" Pattern of Existence
6. Humanity as it is

On this basis, a "Universal Concept of Good and Bad" must be based on the following determinations:

1. When a change in existence is beneficial to any individual and does not harm any other individual, the determination which brought about the change was good.

2. When a change in existence is beneficial to any individual and does harm to any other individual, the determination which brought about the change was bad.

Based on these determinations, the rules of a "Universal Concept of Good and Bad" must limit man to achieve at the expense of <u>nature</u>. An achievement not at the expense of <u>nature</u> must be at the expense of man. Any achievement at the expense of man is harmful to man and is bad by intent.

Any achievement must result in a change in existence which includes man but it may not be at the expense of man. This change in existence must change the achiever directly. This change in existence may change other men either directly or indirectly. Therefore, as man achieves, the changes in existence which he creates must result in changes in man. These changes in man may be to varying degrees of good or bad as determined by their benefit or harm to all men.

Any achievement which benefits man, must be in accordance with the "A" pattern of existence if it is to be within the "Universal Concept of Good and Bad."

Human Relationship Under "Universal Concept of Good and Bad"

Assume that one man accepts the "Universal Concept of Good and Bad." To function in society, he must have some rules to achieve at the expense of <u>nature</u> and not of man. These rules must be in accordance with truth and when followed, the resulting change in existence must harm no one and benefit someone. The rules established on this basis can result in any achievement in accordance with the "A" pattern of existence. Thus this man can overcome the problems of Life Energy, Life Ambient and Life Natural Enemies without making any change in existence which does harm to any other individual. However, he cannot overcome the problems of Life Human Enemies created by the "Three Party System" without making any change in existence which does harm to any other individual. He cannot pay taxes without contributing to a change in existence which does harm to another individual. He cannot refuse to pay taxes and remain a full-fledged member of society. He cannot overcome these problems and he cannot avoid these problems and remain within society. The problem of the "B" pattern of existence and of Life Human Enemies are an inherent part of the "Three Party System" society.

Man can accept but he cannot practice the "Universal Concept of Good and Bad" in a society dominated by the "Three Party System." The only way mankind can ever accept and practice the "Universal Concept of Good and Bad" is to understand and establish the "Two Party System" in all areas and at all levels of control.

The establishment of the "Two Party System" will not assure the acceptance and practice of the "Universal Concept of Good and Bad" by all of mankind. However, if the "Philosophy of Truth" were also accepted, the only variation between controllers would be the variation between brains rather than the variation between races and religions and nations. The variation between controllers' brains would not be a very great incentive to divide mankind against

175

themselves for the purpose of mass self-destruction. With so small an incentive to maintain different concepts of good and bad and so large an incentive to establish a "Universal Concept of Good and Bad," natural selection should rapidly evolve such a concept since it is in the direction of self-preservation.

The establishment of the "Two Party System", the acceptance of the "Philosophy of Truth" and the acceptance of a "Universal Concept of Good and Bad" will not assure the practice of good by all mankind. There are many humans of varying degrees of mental illness who will do harm to fellow humans both by accident and by intent. They are among both controller and controlled. This bad practice will continue until humans conquer the Life Natural Enemies which cause the mental illness.

The Incentive

Assume the establishment of the "Two Party System", the acceptance of the "Philosophy of Truth" and the "Universal Concept of Good and Bad" in an "A" pattern of existence.

What then?

Unlike the spiritual heaven which humans have never been able to conceive or describe in more than two or three meaningless sentences, they could readily create a human heaven which can be described in great detail.

Without the fear, hatred, and frustration of all the old third parties and with an honest understanding that:

> Truth exists
> Truth cannot be created
> Truth must be found

Humans can

> Control the world's population
> Control the world's pollution
> Control the world's soil erosion
> Halt the destruction to extinction of other life forms
> Establish controlled world conservation
> Make desirable living conditions in areas of the world not now desirable
> Conquer disease

   Establish nondestructive world energy sources
   Establish social individual freedom to achieve
   Perhaps find a younger earth

Control of the world's population will inherently increase the quality of life. Control of the world's population will channel all of the increased world product output into a controlled or reduced number instead of an ever expanding number of people. This will rapidly multiply the world standard of living. Beyond this, the acceptance of the "Philosophy of Truth" and the acceptance of the "A" pattern of existence will greatly increase mankind's creativity which must now be directed toward the control of <u>nature</u> rather than the destruction of man. Now the world's standard of living will be such that food, clothing and housing are of no concern. Man's concern will be with his capability and with what good he can achieve within his capability. He will be concerned with what additional truth he can find and prove and use. He will compete creatively and not destructively.

Why is this an incentive?

Because it is a challenge suitable for mankind.

Because when it has been achieved man can say:

   I have come down from the tree
   I have created machines and chemicals
   I have conquered slavery
   I have conquered the "Third Party" superstition
   I have conquered the segregation of brain from brain by material handling systems
   I have conquered the brain's variable capability and established true values
   I have conquered the population explosion of mankind
   I have conquered the evil of man's conquest of man
   I have conquered the sustenance of man
   I have conquered the world and all that is in it
   I have been the salvation of mankind and his world for as long as it last.

And perhaps man can someday say:

   I have conquered space and found other habitable worlds.
   I have been the salvation of man in the universe for as long as it supports man.

When man can say this, he will have become the source of what he is looking for.

This is the incentive.

This future of humanity depends on human ability to acquire true intelligence.

Epilogue

After pondering the limited presentation of the Big Bang Constant Velocity, Uniform Density, Uniform Expansion Concept given in Chapter 14, I realize that this concept deserves much deeper consideration. While this presentation considers only uniform expansion after nucleosynthesis and it makes no change in the development of the red shift (Z) factor's or Hubbell's constant Ho development, it makes a drastic change in the way the universe, expands and what the universe looks like today.

First, to distinguish my concept from the general Big Bang concept, we will call my concept the Long Bang concept since Chart 5 clearly shows the long time required between the maximum force, maximum density, maximum velocity radial emission and the lowest force, lowest density, lowest velocity radial emission. The length of this time could be from the first instigation of the maximum force until there was no force left or until there was a force but no more stuff left. There seems to be a small force left so there you have it.

To contemplate the spherical universe of my concept, it helps to use two time concepts from any point in the universe. One time concept is real time tied to that actual speed of light or photons and the other is an instantaneous time as though the speed of light or photons were infinite. Now, if you will refer to Chapter 14 under Uniformly Decreasing Uniform Universal Density, you will see that it says that maintaining a uniform decreasing universal density and a uniform expansion of all stuff in the universe can take place *simultaneously* under this concept and only under this concept. That means that it can NOT be determined as uniform by viewing under real time except for relatively short distances unless Ho is correct and real time is converted to instantaneous time. Even in instantaneous time, allowance must be made for gravity, which will slow radial expansion in proportion to the distance from the center from the universe. This radial slow down will be equaled by a peripheral expansion slow down of the same order.

We must consider that even without the gravity affect, 88% of the mass of the universe is beyond 50% of its radius and 65% of the mass of the universe is beyond the outer 25% of its radius. This makes a spherical universe quite different from a curved space universe with no center and no edge; especially if the Milky Way is some where in the central part with the QSO's then Quasars populating the outer periphery in all directions as it seems they do.

The latest information I have says the Quasars extend radially to a red shift of over 5 and were therefore over 15 billion light years away when we see them today. So where have they gone in that 15 billion years since the photons we see now left them? How long a time did it take those quasars to get from the location of the Long Bang to where they were when we see them now? They are now receding at 95% of the speed of light. If they went at that speed from the locations of the Long Bang to where we see them now, it would have taken them 15.8 billion light years to get that far. That makes the total age of these outer quasars 30.8 billion years when we see them today.

What of the density of the universe in the 10 to 15 billion light years radius as we see it when it was 10 to 15 billion years old at the present time? All we know of this time and range is what the photons from there tell us. I understand that we can not see even large groups of galaxies at this distance. The reason we can see QSO's and Quasars at this distance is because they are over 100 times brighter than the brightest galaxy and no larger than the solar system. This must mean that their density is tremendous. Even so, there seems to be no real information on the density of the universe at this time and distance and by the Long Bang theory. This should be the density of our part of the universe at about this time. If the density of our part of the universe was as high at this time as the Long Bang theory indicates, any attempt to determine present day age of our part of the universe, without taking the Long Bang time and density into consideration, may not be very accurate.

If my concept of the Long Bang creation is true, and I think it is much more logical than any of the other concepts, then cosmology will have to start over. Of course it may not be true but it is the only concept in accordance with the simple nature of existence where forces move stuff through space in time.